THE PLAYER'S WIVES

A NOVEL BY

CHERISE ARIE

CHERISE ARIE

You must love in such a way that person you love feels free.

-Thich Nhat Hanh

1

B*rrrrriiiiinnnnnggggg!*

STREAKS of orange light slid through the shutters and with the quickness of a snake strike, a hand shot out from under the covers to silence the phone alarm.

Fuck.

Ella wished she could lay in bed all day. She was exhausted from an evening of drifting in and out of slumber. Slowly, she reached her hands towards the headboard and pointed her toes in the opposite direction. Already she could feel the tension of her existence. She averted her eyes towards the other side of the bed, which offered only the slightest evidence of life; the faint sound of air passing through the body and the gentle rise and fall of the blankets. The room was cold, making it even more tempting to retreat into dreamland or a nightmare. Any alternate universe would be better at this point.

Although Ella wasn't alone, she felt lonely. She couldn't help but think about the fallout that would surely come. She was still trying to wrap her mind around the thing that she hadn't even repeated out loud yet.

The night before, Ella had every intention to let Nelly know. The news sat quietly on the tip of her tongue the entire evening. But Nelly barely let her get a word in. She was excited about her podcast and so deep into Neverland, she didn't even read the doom written all over Ella's face. That or Ella was indeed a better actress than she thought. She spent years fooling Ryan that she had somehow transformed into this ideal wife. Yet, in almost three months, she had managed to confuse and destroy love once again. And although this was not new to her, this time was different.

2

(3 MONTHS PRIOR)

The team called Ryan and asked if he could be at the field at 10:00 am. Instantly, he knew it couldn't be good. One, they hadn't ever called him to the field early. Two, they were only a couple of days away from the trade deadline. His agent hadn't mentioned any stirrings of a trade involving him, but he knew in this world, the weather could change with the tide, and tomorrow, he could be packing up his last four years here and starting all over again in a new city.

He got up early to mentally prepare for his next steps. Ella was still sleeping, and although she was not only his wife but an integral part of his representation, he decided he would hold off on alerting her until he knew exactly where they were going. He thought about how this might affect her work considering the move to LA four years prior, skyrocketed her career. This location helped her to service her clients more effectively and partner with several companies that believed in the culture she created with her players. Already, her book of business included over twenty-million in off-the-field deals. A lot of people liked to attribute her success to her husband's connections. Few people knew much about Ella's life before LA to know she had long put her grind in. Ella was a force to be reckoned with and he took notice. It was during her marketing intern days, while finishing up her Master's, that Ryan met her seven years back.

———

RYAN WAS one of the biggest names in professional baseball when he returned to his alma mater for a signing. He walked past Ella working a booth at the event. Initially, he wanted to stop but felt nervous. Her smile was magical, intimidating even, and he could tell that he wasn't the only one to notice. As far as he could see, she had *The Last Dragon* glow and he couldn't help but stare. He was more than glad that his signing booth was at an angle where he could continue to see her. He looked up frequently, Ella never noticing him, but instead holding all of her admirers in the palm of her hand. He was intrigued and couldn't help but to approach her immediately following his required one-hour appearance. He slipped behind some of the booth areas covered partially with tents and snuck up on Ella from behind. The crowd had started to wind down as most people were heading inside for some scheduled performances. Two kids grabbed some of the goodies she had at the tables and they ran off when they had more than they should've.

He waited a few moments before making his presence known. He watched as she picked up the media card for the player's appearance and started smiling when she took a long glance at the photo.

"See something you like?"

He realized he startled her as she turned quickly to see who was behind her and somewhat stuttered out a greeting of sorts. She cleared her throat and jolted herself back into reality. As smoothly as possible, she changed her tune, "Actually, I was wondering how someone so deeply colorful could have the name, Ryan Smith. So, just thinking on a super deep sociological level about slavery, colonization, and stereotypes." Her quick wit made her even more appealing. He flashed the same big, beautiful smile from the photo.

"Oh, she's funny and smart too? We should grab lunch and you could explain this more in-depth to me. Because I can definitely dig a conversation like that."

Her pussy flexed. But so did her soul and she couldn't help but blush. He knew then he had her interest.

"I can't, sorry. Fraternizing is strongly discouraged with players and what not. So, although I'd like to deliver a well-formulated thesis on blackness in America, I will have to decline."

"Ok cool, buuuut... since you'd *like to*, then why don't you go against 'the system' and meet me at Lou's in an hour. From the looks of your skin tone, it looks like you could use a little *color commentary* on that thesis. See you there." He turned and walked away and hoped he was exuding the same confidence as her and prayed that it would work.

"WHAT THE FUCK WAS THAT?" she said out loud to herself and started cleaning out her booth. A sensation moved through her body that she hadn't felt in years. Ella was no stranger to romantic attention but made zero time for meaningful relationships, instead opting for a roll around with snacks that weren't meant to be had for meals. Her career was her lover and she was loyal to it.

Her supervisor walked over. "Leaving?"

"Yea, I'm not feeling so great. Going to head out early. Not much of a turn out anyway. I'll see you first thing tomorrow?"

"Alright, Ella. Great job today. You acquired quite a few admirers from the alumni group." Unphased, she managed her toothy flawless, seemingly flattered smile and gathered her belongings.

Ella felt a sudden urge to entice her suitor. She caught a cab to her apartment, as this was a dire situation that was a cause for dire measures, even though every dime was needed else-where that month. It was merely coincidental that she lived a short five-minute walk from the restaurant, so she damn near sprinted the three flights to her apartment, anxious to look sexy. She decided against heels for a casual lunch and opted for cute sandals that accentuated her freshly painted red toes and her favorite long, somewhat see-through summer dress. She pulled the hair tie from her bun releasing her thick beautiful tresses almost to the ledge of her ass. With her morning make-up still intact, she quickly applied a soft red color to her 'thick slick' lips. In ten minutes' time, she had freshened up and transformed her look completely. She paused in the mirror before leaving. She loved the way this dress gave the slightest tease of her breasts. It always turned her on. The flower pattern was just enough disguise to make it acceptable that she wasn't wearing a bra. She looked at the time. It had already been just over an hour since she left the campus.

When she turned the corner, she was surprised to see Ryan outside of the restaurant but quickened her stride thinking maybe he was leaving since it had been fifteen minutes past the hour. Once she was in his line of sight, she slowed down her walk and pretended to be busy on her phone. The next time she looked up, he was staring at her with a boyish grin. It was like the boy in middle school that managed some impressive physical feat only to look at his crush and realize she was watching. The way his lips outlined his shining white teeth was almost too much to bear. The color white never looked better on anyone as far as she could tell.

"And just when I thought the sun couldn't shine any brighter." Ryan opened the door for her and took a full inventory as she walked in. Ella made a gesture as if she was flattered, but clearly, she knew what she was doing. He wanted to touch her hair, smell her neck, and run his fingertips across her golden bronze skin. He took a deep breath to redirect his thoughts and they were quickly seated.

The conversation was like water, flowing back and forth without much effort. Ella wanted to lick every word that dripped from his lips. He was funny, smart, and made no secret that he was enjoying her presence. He ordered the food for the table and winked at her to trust him. It was a gesture that might have upset her, but his choices were perfect and she for once didn't mind someone else taking control.

After they ate, Ryan had to head straight to the airport. He'd only flown in for the appearance, and although he wished he could stay longer, he had to get back to Atlanta for a previous commitment.

"You look much too delicious to be walking down these streets on this glorious afternoon." He waved down a cab for her and handed a fifty to the driver. He opened her door but then got in her way. "Just so you know, I'm going to marry you, Ella."

Ella smacked her lips and laughed. "Well, I certainly hope this isn't your proposal. Besides, I might have too much sauce for you."

"Really. You think I would bring you to a Jamaican restaurant if I didn't like my shit spicy."

RYAN WASN'T BLUFFING. He moved her to Atlanta a few months later when she graduated and became her first client. She got at it right away, and within months, one of Ryan's teammates hired her for marketing as well. From there, she acquired a few other clients but always kept Ryan as her main focus.

Ella paced her career to create space and support for him to thrive. Her mom advised her early that being married would make her more credible and respected in that industry so she didn't hesitate when he wanted to get married shortly after her move. She worked hard to build connections in Atlanta as she wasn't well-received by just quite everyone there. When Ryan was on fire, it made her job easier, and with her as his inspiration, it made getting hot easier. They complimented each other like a see-saw, each one doing what they had to, to help the other one go higher. When he became a free agent, they were both convinced that an offer in LA was just what they needed to take them to the next level—but Los Angeles had been waiting anxiously for Ella. Her career took off faster than either one of them could've predicted, and it instantly affected Ryan. His first season playing in LA was the worst of his career. He played much better in the subsequent season, but since then it was hard for him to demonstrate a better athlete than when he signed the deal.

Maybe a new start was what they both needed. Maybe he would be sent to a city where Ella could scale back a bit. Then he could revisit the discussion about kids. At this point in her career, it wasn't even something she wanted to hear, but he thought maybe moving to a smaller setting would make her start to think about it.

Those were selfish thoughts. He started feeling guilty about riding her tail as of late, allowing gossip and his insecurities to lead him to lightly accuse her of getting too friendly with some of the players. It was a ridiculous accusation, with him knowing above all others that Ella's career was her focus and her professionalism was everything to her.

His phone went off and suddenly he realized he had reminisced for way too long. He decided to leave without saying bye.

WHEN RYAN ARRIVED at the stadium, he parked and walked briskly past the security guards. He knew them all well and usually would stop for some brief chatter, but he didn't want them to start asking why he was there. He wore his headphones down into the tunnel and straight to the team room, just giving friendly head nods along the way to some of the groundskeepers. He set his bag down in his locker and headed to the AGM's office. Bill was already walking in his direction.

"Ryan, my man. I was just headed to grab some water. Walk with me. Just waiting on Rick and Jose to come down. They're on their way." They headed back towards the team room. For the first time since his call-up to the big leagues, he felt small in these underground hallways. Being there almost every day for the past few years had made him immune to the enormity of it all. But now, as the possibility of leaving lingered over his head, anxiety managed to fill up the entire tunnel-like smoke. Was he being sent down? Traded? Released? He tried to remain calm and appear confident. Bill knew how these things went. He was a player once too. He tried to lighten the mood. "How's the wife? I saw Trevino in that BMW commercial and I heard that was a pretty sweet deal she got him over there."

"Yeah man, you know Ella. She stay doing her thing." They were almost back at Bill's office so Ryan decided to cut to the chase. "Speaking of her, what's up Bill? Where am I headed? You know Ella really got a lot going on here."

"Oh, you're not leaving Ryan. Just moving a few things around." The place was so empty, they could hear walking and talking coming from around the corner. "That's them now. Let's have a seat." The General Manager and the Coach came in just behind them.

"Rick, Ryan thought we were trading him so let's not waste any time."

All three men turned towards Ryan as Rick started speaking. "Ryan, this organization loves you and we respect you, so we are just going to cut straight to the chase. We've been looking for a way to free up some money and last night we were presented with an opportunity that does just that. We've acquired Tres Dominguez in a deal. He's a bit of a mess off the field, but he's hot right now and we think adding him to the roster immediately can give us a good chance getting to the postseason. This isn't a permanent move, just looking to try some things out. This will give you some time to rehab your shoulder. In the meantime, you'll be getting some at-bats as needed."

A pinch hitter. It was like a punch from behind. His pride, already struggling, completely disappeared into an abyss. He could only manage to say, "Wow, definitely wasn't expecting that."

3

"Nelly, hear me out. What's gotten into you? I mean. Not like that. I'm just saying, split?" He was stumbling over his words. Nelly's behavior was scaring him. She had been calm and stoic since pics and video of him surfaced on The Shade Room showing him at a party getting cozy with some "influencer." And that wasn't the worst part. He left with the chick, got pulled over and arrested for a DUI. The team already considered trading him before this incident. He had been warned a few times to keep his nose clean, but with this type of negative publicity, they wanted him gone immediately.

No one could deny his impact on the field, and two back-to-back All-Star designations were enough for several teams to express interest. John, his agent, called him first thing in the morning to inform him that the team had finalized a deal with LA. The team called shortly after to confirm. His flight had been booked for the evening and John wanted to know when or if he should send Nelly and the kids. John had known Tres since he was a kid. He was a close friend and former teammate of his father. He knew the game in every sense of the word, but more importantly, he knew Tres and Nelly's relationship. This wasn't their first rodeo, but he did know that in this lifestyle, sometimes the women decided to tap out after one too many "incidents." And this time, that's exactly what Nelly was thinking. She could only imagine Tres in Los Angeles, an exclusive hub for his favorite type of woman to fuck on. More than anything, privacy was what she craved and she knew LA was the furthest thing from it.

"I already told John to book your flight with mine." He was lying.

"Well, tell him to cancel it." She was sitting on the edge of the bed. He walked into the closet and grabbed both their suitcases. He set them on the bed, continuing to plead. "Damn baby, for real? It's like that? I know you're upset right now. I fucked up. But you just going to leave me that easily. After everything we've been through?"

"I get it. I am forever indebted to you. You saved me. If it wasn't for you, who knows where I would be. For the millionth time. This is my lot and I should just be grateful."

"That's not what I'm saying, mami." He approached her and sat down right beside her. He tried to be gentle in his physique. Nelly glanced towards the floor, feeling overwhelmed at his proximity.

"I'm tired Tre. I really, *really* don't care what you do with these women, but I'm tired of trying to figure out what persona to give the outside world. It's exhausting. And quite honestly, I thought you would have calmed down by now. I mean, my God, el hombre insatiable."

"Damn, Nelly. That's not fair." Nelly rolled her eyes and got up. She walked towards the window to her favorite spot in the penthouse. He searched quickly for better words. "But you're right. I don't know why I still act so immature. For real though. This move is what we need. I can see that. And I am older now. I never really think about the reality of losing you, but I can't Nelly. You really are the only person I trust in this whole world and you know that. I mean how can I even face this new venture without you. I would just crumble. Y los niños, baby? We all need you. We all need to be together. Y tú sabe."

Nelly continued staring out of the bedroom window. This particular spot offered sweeping views of Lake Erie and the skyline. The ever-changing panorama provided respite from her external chaos and helped her sort out her thoughts. She knew he was telling the truth about only trusting her. They had been best friends in high school, and aside from a multi-million dollar contract, he hadn't changed too much. Tres continued, "I know I keep saying it, but I do need to talk to someone. You know professionally. We both went through that shit as kids, and I don't know, maybe that's why I can't control myself."

He was looking for her usual compassion. But, over the years she had come to believe that everyone suffered from some form of sexual trauma in their youth, so that excuse was getting old. He had sung this song too many times before and he could tell she was no longer dancing.

"Nelly, baby, I will do whatever you want. Please. What do you want? What do you need? At least just come with me tonight. Your sister can stay with the kids, and I can even fly your mom in if you want. Just come with me tonight so we can talk more privately and I will support whatever you want to do."

Tres genuinely wanted to change and support her better. It was just that the puffed-up exaggeration of his importance took up too much of his energy to be able to grow towards anyone but himself. His success was his master, and he was bound to its perils.

Nelly stood silently for longer than a moment. Her sister, Selena, and her two kids were in town visiting and had planned on being there for the next few weeks right up until the start of school. Nelly knew Selena would not have any problem staying there while she went to sort things out, and she knew her kids would be unbothered in her absence during their cousin time. She finally turned towards Tres. He sat on the edge of the bed still. His herculean stature looked as if it was melting right before her eyes. He held the same pain is his expression from the day she met him. She could always see it in him. There were times, when only for a passing moment, it would seem as if he finally healed. But then she would be quickly snatched back into reality by his fucking habit. Most times, his escapades weren't an issue. However, every once in a while an opportunistic Instagrammer would be extra dehydrated and looking for the slightest bit of attention. It was those hoes that got under her skin. The ones so thirsty, they were willing to step on another woman's toes to get what they wanted. Humping on her husband behind closed doors was 100% the responsibility of him, but putting it out there for the world to see, that was hoe shit. His foolishness in dealing with those types was frustrating. It made him look like a weak ass wounded lion, pitiful even.

She started to walk out of the room, but first said without expression, "I'll go, but I need space."

She found Selena and the kids in the playroom. "I'm going to head to LA tonight with Tres. Not sure how long, but I can have Mom come help."

"Help with what? These kids entertain each other all day and damn near feed themselves. I think I can handle it." Selena knew exactly what her sister was going through. "I know what you don't need is mom in your ear right now, telling you how to feel and excusing his behavior. Go take care of your business sis, I got this." Nelly hugged her, squeezing tight enough to train the tears to remain deep behind her eyes. She whispered a thank you and headed to pack.

4

Tre's entrance into the locker room was as bright and loud as the streets during Christmas time in the Dominican Republic. His jeans gripped his juicy turkey leg looking thighs and squeezed tighter as they went down to his ankles where they were met by some fur-lined Gucci slippers. If the shoes weren't already enough, a matching belt sat somewhat quietly at the bottom of his tucked-in shirt, technically a blouse by the looks, with only the last few buttons connected. His gold chains looked pleased to be resting on his lightly tanned chest, full of pride and confidence upon first impression. If you didn't know any better, his cockiness seemed charming. Everything about this papi chulo looked as if a full band would appear as the guido started, and he would grab the mic from his back pocket and pour out a steamy bachata ballad.

If the sight of him wasn't enough, his fragrance dominated the air space. Of course with his shades still on, he searched the room for a friendly face. Once he turned in the direction of Jaime Sanchez, he stopped, looked down through the top of his glasses, then posed with his arms outstretched. Of course they knew each other. They were essentially twins. Both out of New York, both sons of the game.

"Que lo que, manito." Sanchez shouted across the room. Most of the guys were wearing headphones and in their pre-game zone, including Ryan. A few turned around to see what the commotion was about.

"Tú sabe." Tres headed to him, flashing a smile and throwing a few head nods to the guys he didn't know personally.

"Bienvenido, Los Angeles. La tierra de leche y miel." Jaime reached his hand out and pulled Tres in for a hug, welcoming him to the land of milk and honey. He motioned for a couple of his teammates to introduce them. Tres didn't know everyone by name and face, but they knew him. Within seconds the entire pack was erupting with laughter and some derivative of Spanish and English. A few other guys made their way over for a quick greeting.

Even though Ryan remained facing his locker with noise cancellers purposefully secured to his ears, he knew Tres was in the room. He was still deciding how to approach him. He had seen his jersey two lockers away right when he got there, so he knew he would have to say something eventually. He also knew the other guys would be watching him. These types of situations were always awkward, and some handled it better than others. Ryan could feel the energy settle back down and new it would be seconds before Tres was within a few feet of him. This was the moment of truth. Ryan slid his headphones down to his neck and turned his body towards Tres.

"Hey man." He gave his best enthusiasm. "Welcome to the organization. We're really focused on getting to the postseason and I'm hearing you can help with that."

"Oh yea, man. For sure. I mean that's my goal. Appreciate it." He was pleasant.

Ryan stood and walked towards him, lowering his voice.

"Look man, just a heads up. Coach is a little more low key. I like your style, but the organization isn't always fond of your 'man-ito' over there. Do your thing, for sure, but try to make it as much about ball as possible."

"Good looking out brotha. Tres Dominguez." It was a humble and unnecessary introduction, just an attempt to show respect.

"Yep." He extended his hand.

Tres grabbed it with both hands and then released one to his heart. "I'm a fan Ryan. When I first got called up, I was gunning for a rookie season like yours. Mucho respect my brother." Ryan was impressed. He did have a historic rookie year, but he figured Tres was at least five to six years younger than him. A player with his prominence in high school would be more concerned with himself, and maybe some of the All-Stars. Ryan was just starting to make a name for himself at that time, but in the world of baseball enthusiasts, he had long been the man.

"My dad played, you know, so he made me study the best."

"Thanks man. That means a lot. Get your gear, you're in my group. We up first." The team was strategic in having Tres and Ryan do batting practice together. They held Ryan in high esteem and hoped he would be able to move beyond his ego to mentor Tres. Ryan was being groomed for coaching. At thirty-three, he was on the last leg of his career. He had a great reputation around the league and he had the educational background that could help land him in a front-office position if he played his cards right. Ryan was aware of all this, he just didn't expect it so soon.

They chatted it up on the field as they waited their turns and Ryan hated that he found Tres pretty likable. His enthusiasm reminded him of himself at that age, when most players are in their prime. He made sure to display some Godly forms of power every few swings of the wood, but Tres managed to keep up. Ryan knew that keeping him close could play to his advantage. After practice, they exchanged numbers.

"I'm sure they told you about the charity event Saturday night. Plan on attending it, it's the owner's annual thing. Bring Nelly, I'll introduce her to Ella."

5

They hadn't been in LA but a few days before Tres asked Nelly to join him at a charity event for the team. She reminded him that he was supposed to be giving her space, but he promised this would be the only thing he needed her to attend just to show face and appear as a united front to the organization. He did his best to act normal from the time they left Cincinnati although her demeanor baffled him. She had been pleasant, yet short in her interactions with him. Secretly, he was hoping they could have a fun night out. The kids weren't coming for another couple of weeks and time alone always helped them rekindle. She decided to go. Even though it was last minute, the idea of a few drinks was appealing. Her alone time had consisted of pampering and shopping so she was more than ready to subtly show out. They hadn't been out anywhere together in months so she was in rare form, dressed beyond sexy just to get to him.

They arrived at the venue around eight in the evening in a custom-wrapped matte black Maserati Gran Turismo. The few guests standing outside turned towards the pure purr of the engine when Tres pulled up. Tres hopped out and ran to the passenger door before the valet had a chance. Nelly could always capture the attention of a crowd, especially when dressed like this, and Tres wanted to be the one to present her. He extended his hand toward her and she delicately placed her fingers in his. It was the most they had touched in a while and it sent chills through his body. He wished to nestle in her softness and longed for the comfort she always provided. But she offered no consolation in her body language. Still, he placed her hand and arm in his and kept it there as they walked.

They paused for a red carpet photo before proceeding towards what appeared to be a large warehouse. Inside had been transformed into a Bellagio-Esque casino floor. The event had started at six, and everyone that was expected was already there. The guests were dressed to the nines, a black-tie gala indeed. Nelly's dress was scandalous in comparison and she thought it rather fitting. She wore that shit like her own skin and stood poised, body looking right, chin high. The sight of them attracted the looks of many. Upon spotting the bar, Nelly pressed the tips of her Givenchy heels into the floor and tugged at his arm where hers was intertwined to indicate she wanted to separate, but not without a kiss. She too knew how to play the game, but he knew she needed a drink to warm up first. He met her lips and pointed to where he would be. He watched her walk away before turning to head towards some of the guys.

"Patron margarita on the rocks." Even the bartender had noticed her entrance and winked with the deliberate long pour.

"Sugar or salt?"

"Ain't shit sweet." A sly smile slid across her face.

"That could be disputed." It was a respectful compliment, just to let her know she was seen. "Let me know when you want another."

She turned to scope the crowd and noticed some ladies headed her way. She turned to the bar and threw down the rest of her drink, and signaled the bartender for another.

"Hi. Mrs. Talia Douglas. " Nelly turned around after grabbing her second drink. Talia extended her hand and flashed a smile as bright and big as her ring and the rest of her jewelry.

"And Mrs. Kimberly Jones." She did the same. They were both dressed in rather conservative black cocktail dresses, yet fully adorned with jewels and fancy little clutches. Everything about them, including introductions with titles, let her know these were the women to be careful of.

"I'm Mrs. Chanel Dominguez, but everyone just calls me Nelly." She knew to keep it cool and play dumb, but she was feeling a little buzzed, thus froggy. These were the veteran wives, and if one of them decided to try her, she would make sure to leap.

"Well, you can call me T and we call her Kim. We were just seeing what club you belonged to. This is the wives club, aka the Main Course, aka the Hive. Over there you got the appetizers or the groupies, and the side dishes are over there scattered about. You can spot the wives in their respective cliques, in pretty close vicinity to their husbands."

Nelly glanced around the room and could clearly see what they were talking about. She appreciated the welcome committee but didn't want to be stuck talking with wives all night. There was a chance they knew about her husband's recent episode and would find some way to make a backhanded comment. She did her best to appear like she was looking for someone, but they kept right on talking.

"You don't look like a rookie so I'm sure you can tell the difference. Anyway, we'd like to invite you to the meeting of the Hive. We always like to formally welcome new wives to the team and provide resources to help them get acclimated here. Although Kim and I have never dealt with a trade ourselves, we have seen first-hand how tough it can be. Kids?"

"Yes, two."

"Oh, well we will get you information on schools and

nannies right away. Our dear Mrs. Jessica Siths oversees that department."

"Who's that?" Something, or someone rather, caught Nelly's attention.

"Oh, she's not here. Ironically enough, she didn't have someone to watch her kids this..."

Nelly interrupted, "No, her?"

Talia and Kim turned to see the small group of older executive men that had her attention and then realized why. There in the center, pulling them all under her spell was Ella Smith. They were a bit annoyed by her lack of interest in their new wife orientation.

"*Her*?" They both did the type of fake laugh that was riddled with jealousy. "That's Ella Smith. She's a wife, but she has a group of her own, with little to no members. She's far too busy with the players to have time for the Hive activities or any of the women groups for that matter. As you can see, she likes to spend her time around the guys." T and Kim glanced at each other and rolled their eyes in conjunction with slick, familiar smiles.

Nelly took a sip of her drink. These were the ones who had arranged marriages. They came from money and families that believed these unions to be cornerstones of their wealth and assurance that it would stay. These women would be guaranteed security and highly protected from divorce or even scandal. Their husbands paid far too much for sex and with a select clientele that they wouldn't run that risk. What these women didn't have were their freedom and voice. That's why they had the loudest bark and snipped at anyone woman "allowed" to roam freely, especially when married.

Nelly had been around these women far too long. She knew most likely, that Ella just wasn't the type to clique up with the mean girls. Those girls—women like Ella that is—always got called hoes by the "better ones."

Nelly watched Ella as they talked shit. She could barely process anything they were saying. She remembered Tres telling her about one of the player's wives that worked in the industry and guessed it might be her. There was something so attractive about her in the way she commanded the attention of everyone around her. T and Kim's chatter faded into the background as Nelly's gaze locked eyes with Ella. It only lasted a second, but the jolt of waves it sent through the women was undeniable. Ella returned her attention to her audience, but couldn't help to shake the feeling that they had already met Nelly turned back into her crowd of two, ready to make her exit.

"Here's my number. I'd love to meet the other ladies. Tres is waving me over. Excuse me." He could see from across the room that she was looking for an escape route. He preferred she didn't get too close with any of the women. It was always messy and led to tension.

Nelly started to walk towards Tres when a woman pretended to accidentally bump her.

"Oh, excuse me. Nelly Dominguez right? My friend, Tara, knows your husband."

"I'm sure she does. Tre can't seem to fill his cup when it comes to nuts if you know what I mean?" The woman looked confused. Nelly glanced at her ring finger, "Ok, maybe you don't. Anyway I hope you hit the jackpot one of these days so you don't have to keep pulling on so many levers. Time is money in this world honey and you don't have a lot of it left. How old are you, like 35? Almost time to leave the cleat chasing to ones that have the energy. If you ain't hit by now, I just don't know. Oh, and tell your friend I said hi." The woman looked like a deer in the headlights. It was a bit much, but at this point she didn't give a fuck. She didn't care who knew her husband and she wasn't interested in how.

Nelly didn't even wait for her to reply. She continued

walking towards Tres who was now standing with Ella and Ryan.

"Baby, I want you to meet Ryan and his wife Ella."

ELLA LOOKED up from her phone and paused for what seemed like forever. She felt a strange surge through her abdomen and managed a smile.

Shit, damn, motherfucker, she sang in her head. She was taken aback by the sight of her. "Where do I know you from?"

"I don't think we've ever met. People always tell me I have one of those familiar faces." Nelly smiled softly. Ella was stuck, unbeknownst to the guys, staring. In part, she was trying to figure out where she had seen her before. Nelly had her hand extended, "Chanel, but everyone calls me Nelly." Ella met her hand and as she made contact the need between her legs made her tighten her pussy muscles.

"It's nice to meet you Chanel. Welcome to the organization. I saw you already got acquainted with some of the ladies. You'll find they're just as lovely here as any other ball club."

"Yes, I've noticed. Quite lovely." They both smiled as Nelly was picking up what she was putting down. But more than the smile, there was this unusual vibe. Ella wondered if maybe she was imagining the way Nelly seemed to be looking at her.

"Yea Nelly's a bit anti-social. But from what Ryan told me, you seem like the type of gal she could get along with." She looked away towards the bar in an effort to ignore Tres talking like he was introducing his child at a playdate. She changed the subject.

"You drink? I can use another."

"Actually yes, great idea. I've been working non-stop today." Ella replied eagerly.

As they walked towards the bar, Ryan winked at Tres and

they went to join some of the guys. Nelly and Ella spotted a little section near the bar, away from the crowd. As they went to sit, their legs gently grazed each other causing a static shock. Nelly jumped a bit and then giggled. Ella smiled cooly, "Damn, you electric." Nelly laughed harder. She was definitely feeling her drinks, but Ella was making her feel all tingly. She motioned for the bartender as she tried to gather herself.

"So I hear you work in the industry, marketing right? That sounds exciting!"

"Sounds can be deceiving."

"Everything can be deceiving." Nelly regretted that statement immediately. She didn't know if Ella knew anything about Tres and his shenanigans, but wanted all of that to be the farthest from her mind. "You have kids?"

"No. You?"

"Yes, two. Sorry, hope that question didn't offend you. I'm just always looking for a mom I can tolerate for play dates."

"You didn't offend me. I get asked that question a lot. I don't have any problem saying I'm too focused on my career and myself to have kids right now. Not to say that a woman can't be focused on her career with kids, but that's not how I would prefer to do it. Honestly, I've never even imagined myself with kids. I don't know. To each her own, right?" She held her glass out and Nelly met it with hers. They both threw back the glass.

"Well, I will tell you this much, when and if you do have kids, you will cherish evenings like this when you can reach out to the old you, before kids, and awaken that young, wild spirit for just a few hours." Nelly chuckled and Ella called over the bartender.

"Another round for a night off."

"Two weeks actually. The kids are finishing up a summer program in Cleveland, so I intend to have few evenings like this." Nelly was already hoping she would get to hang with Ella again and wanted her to know she would be available.

As they chatted away, Ella was surprised at how easy it was to talk to Nelly. The ladies were right; she barely made acquaintance with any of the wives, and only occasionally engaged in conversations with girlfriends and groupies, a major faux pas by their standards. The ease made her curious and she started to take inventory of Nelly. Her complexion resembled liquid milk chocolate, smooth and flawless. Her lips were small but full. Her curly dark hair landed below her shoulders as to tease her breasts. She was petite yet curvaceous in a skinny thick way. As beautiful as she was, it wasn't that. Ella was around beautiful women quite often. But when she reached her almond-shaped eyes, she realized that was what was drawing her in. Nelly's light brown eyes penetrated right into Ella and made no secret that she was feeling some type of way. Somehow in this room full of people, she could feel Nelly's energy and desire.

MEANWHILE, the fellas were going pretty hard themselves. A few of the players were watching Ryan closely. He was a veteran guy and how he responded could make the difference in how they viewed him. The night before, Ryan had an opportunity to pinch-hit and hit a two-run homer. It was a reminder to all, including himself, that he was not to be easily dismissed.

While Tres looked like the life of the party, on the inside he couldn't stop thinking about what Nelly meant about space. In an attempt to quiet the thoughts, he continued to throw back shots. Ryan wasn't much of a drinker, but was trying to keep up. The guys were doing their regular spiel, exaggerating and trying to crack on each other. As the event was starting to wind down, Tres was just getting super amped. He had way too much energy for the night to end. "You and Ella should come over to our place. We don't have much inside yet, but we do have somewhere to sit and drinks. It's right up the street."

"Sounds good to me. I'll go get the misses."

Ryan was feeling pretty drunk, but it felt good. He was thinking about Ella and feeling bad still for giving her shit. He was hoping she was having a good time and that he could find a way to patch things up. When he spotted her, she was full of smiles and he smiled too, thinking he hadn't seen Ella so lax in a long time. He snuck up behind her. "Hey baby." He put his arms on her shoulders and kissed her cheek. Startled by the interruption, she almost pulled away, but kept her form. Nelly looked away and reached in her purse for her phone.

"What time is it anyway? It's getting late." She turned around to look for Tres.

"Oh, you should know Tres just invited us over, but I can decline if you're feeling tired." Nelly couldn't grasp the idea. She didn't want the night to end with Ella, but the reality of Tres being in the picture made her think twice.

"Oh, that's fine. We don't have much at the house except somewhere to sit and some drinks."

Ryan laughed, "Y'all two are really a match. Tres just said the exact same thing. We'll follow y'all then?" He instructed them to come by grabbing Ella's hand. Ella didn't stand when he tugged.

"I don't know about you guys, but we are in no position to drive," Ella stated, not sure she wanted to have a double date.

"What you talking about woman, we good, besides Tres said they are right up the street in the Hills. They aren't far from us." And against their better judgment, they drove the fifteen minutes up into the Hollywood Hills to a secluded estate with views overlooking the city. The car rides were fairly quiet, as they were all floating in their alcohol. They pulled into the driveway, and Tres got out first to open the front door and went straight for a bottle. He turned towards the others as they came in, with the bottle in hand.

"What should we cap it off with, Patron?"

"Patron is dangerous," Ella said.

"Patron it is." Nelly walked to grab four glasses.

Tres put some music on and everyone threw down two shots each.

"I'm done." Ella waved her hand, feeling the heat travel anxiously to meet the heat coming up from her root.

"Awww, you scared El?" Ryan said.

"I'm not going to put myself in a situation." Ella laughed, but with warning.

"Y'all should kiss." Tres blurted out. He was oblivious to Ryan for a moment. In his stupor, he was eyeing Ella. He heard about her but never really bumped shoulders with her before. This was the first time he was up close and personal.

"You're drunk," Nelly said it to Tres, but then cut her eyes towards Ella also. The sexual tension was rising like a rocket.

"I'm sure Ella would love that, man." Ryan was staring at Ella, picturing the same as Tres. The liquor had them all by the balls.

Ella glanced at Nelly, and she only looked pleased, which made her want to forget any inhibitions and lean into her swiftly and softly. But Ella knew better.

"Let's get going, Ryan. Y'all outta control." She got up and started for the door, looked back seductively at Ryan, bit her lip, and motioned for him to follow.

"That's my cue, and I'm taking it." He got up quickly and followed and Ella could see his bulge down to the left of his fitted jeans, begging to come out. She knew they wouldn't make it five minutes down the road before he released all that freak.

When they got in the car, Ryan grabbed his dick through his jeans.

"You see this, baby. This is for you. You want to suck it?"

He opened his jeans and pulled it out. "Come here, open your mouth baby. You wanted to eat her pussy? I know you did. Put this in your mouth and touch yourself." He put the car in reverse and started to drive. He kept one hand on the wheel and reached the other over to grab a handful of her ass. Her mind flooded with thoughts of Nelly.

She closed her eyes and imagined Nelly on the receiving end of her tongue and let her lips open slowly along Ryan's tip. He moaned. After about forty-five seconds, he quickly pulled over. He grabbed a handful of Ella's hair and used all his strength to pull gently as he came inside her mouth.

"You the best baby."

She opened the door to spit, wiped her mouth and replied, "I know."

NELLY CRAWLED into bed soon after Ryan and Ella left, leaving Tres blue. Her night was over and she longed for the privacy to touch herself and think of Ella.

6

"That was some wild shit last night." Ryan was just waking up. It was early, but later than usual for both of them to still be laying in bed.

"Yea it was." Ella almost thought he was reading her mind as she imagined what the kiss would've been like. "We were so drunk, we definitely shouldn't have drove. I barely remember much after we left the event."

"Well, it was just nice to spend some time with you, even if you don't remember it." His tone changed and there was a hint of spite in his voice.

"Here you go." Ella rolled her eyes, took a deep breath, and sat up to swing her feet to the floor. The hangover made her pause before standing.

"I didn't mean anything by it. But if we are being honest, it seems like you saving the leftovers for me lately."

"What is that supposed to mean?" Ella walked into the bathroom which was still too close to his lecture for her liking.

"All I'm saying is you've been super busy with your 'clients'. Last night was the first time we hung out in a while and it's been even longer since we've had sex, especially like that."

"Really, Ryan? You're going to start this shit again. Must I remind you that you're the one that pushed me to sign Johnson and Enriques, knowing they were high maintenance. You know firsthand that my plate is fucking full. When I'm not working, I try to split my time between you and resting, which usually just gets combined into one. I mean, do you ever think I could use some time to myself that doesn't include work or you?" She turned on the faucet to splash water on her face and filled up a glass to swallow two aspirin.

"I guess I didn't realize you needed time without me, considering we already spend a lot of time apart."

"That's not what I'm saying Ryan. Don't turn me into a villain. You know I'm busting my ass to build something for us for when you're not playing anymore. Obviously, it's not the most secure job." She knew she was taking a jab.

"Wow. You sure sound like a villain Ella." He finally got out of the bed and headed towards the closet. "But anyway, I'm headed to the children's hospital for the toy drive you organized for me. I'm guessing you forgot because you haven't reminded me, nor do you look like you're going."

"Shit. Let me get dressed."

"It's cool Ella. Thank you for just keeping me relevant. It's clear I will be one of your lower maintenance players at least for now. You just focus on Enriques. He's hot right now. Or better yet, why don't you use the day to get some much needed time for yourself."

He got ready quickly and left without her, slamming the door on the way out and turning up his music in his car loud enough for her to hear inside. Ella knew he was being facetious, and hoped that a drive, by himself would cool him down. The past few weeks were made up of conversations similar to this one. Ryan knew how much she worked and how much she tried to be there for him at the same time, yet he was complaining about how much time she was spending with Joe

Enriques, who had just done All-Star and was making a successful crossover into Hollywood. There were rumors that they were getting cozy, which was farthest from the truth, but Ryan had the nerve to address those rumors with her as if he was starting to question them himself. Over the years, several people tried testing their relationship and asked Ryan why he would let his wife work in this business. He always blew them off for the most part, because Ella never gave him a reason not to trust her. Ryan was going through something, it showed on the field and in his numbers. His batting average plummeted and he was making more errors than usual. Off the field, he had been picking fights with her and trying to make her feel bad every chance he got. Ella had tried talking to him about it, and even suggested a session with a good sports psychologist she knew. Ryan insisted it was a normal slump and it angered him for her to suggest otherwise. She left it alone when he began blaming her and her lack of attention for his frustrations. That only made her more aloof. When news of the demotion came, they were already existing in a bad space, and that made it worse. She thought the blow job in the car would relieve some of his tensions, but from the conversation, he was still going through it. And understandably so. At the same time, she wasn't willing to take the hits for his demons since she knew exactly what this particular demon was.

She threw herself together and made her way to the hospital. Ryan needed her, even if it peeved him to admit it. Ella was a master at keeping business and pleasure, or lack thereof, on two separate planets. But Ryan kept that same energy towards her at the event, saying but two words to her during the one hour visit. He was all smiles for the children and the cameras and she maintained the illusion that everything was grand in paradise.

"Hɪ Mᴏᴍ." Ella finally answered her mother's call on the drive home from the hospital. She had been calling for the last three days, ever since news of the trade broke and Ryan had been benched. Ella knew exactly what the conversation would be, which is why she hadn't answered.

"Ella! I've been calling you honey. How are you? How's Ryan?" The second question was the one she was interested in.

"Well Mom, I'm ok, just juggling the clients, trying to keep everyone happy, which is a circus act in and of itself."

"Oh, I know it. But you're so good at it. You always have been honey. And Ryan, how's he handling his situation? I was wondering why y'all haven't called me. Dad told me he's pinch-hitting. Isn't that just something? That team is just always wanting to try a new flavor." Ella was barely listening, indulging her mother by allowing her to go on and on. "I mean I read about this Tres guy. What kind of name is that—the number three. I mean he is just so extra, and disrespectful. Whew, chile, I saw that mess about him and that girl. Oh, his poor wife. He is quite the eye candy, but my oh my, you can't let *everybody* have a taste. I'm glad Ryan hit it out on Friday. Maybe he can knock some damn sense back into management." She wanted to get in as much as possible before Ella found a way to end the call.

"Yea Mom. Ryan will be alright. You know it's time to start exploring some other avenues anyway. Not that he's ready to hang up the cleats. He still has plenty to give, but it's good for a player of his caliber to get a little rest here and there in his career, allowing for his longevity."

"You're always so positive Ella. That's why everyone loves you. Just like when you were little, you could put a smile on anyone's face. Well, I'm happy to hear that you aren't worried, and that you and Ryan are both doing just fine. That makes me feel so much better. And please honey, don't ignore my calls for so many days. It just drives me crazy. I know you got it all under control, but sometimes I just need to hear it out of your mouth. Tell Ryan I love him, and maybe I will come see y'all soon."

"Ok Mom, that sounds good. Love you."

"Love you too."

Ella told her Mom exactly what she wanted to hear, as always, which wasn't to say much, just a few comforting words and mostly listen to her assume everything was dandy.

She pulled into a juice bar close to the house and figured she would handle some emails and respond to texts. She had a few hours before she was needed at a Panini signing event for another one of her clients. She didn't have the energy to outshine Ryan's darkness, so she would just immerse herself in her work, as always, the best excuse to detach from anything real. Sunday was the one day they tried to carve out time for each other. There were a lot of early games on Sundays and Ella could try to schedule work around that day. But it was clear that her presence agitated him, so she would just keep to herself. She was stressed too, but that never seemed to be of importance. She was always expected to be the support.

She looked down at her phone to start sifting through texts and emails. There was a message from an unknown number.

Nelly: Ella! I got your number from Tiffany. Hope you don't mind. You available today by any chance? I was wondering if you would like to meet out for a coffee or something.

Ella: Who is this?

Nelly: Sorry, this is Nelly, Tres Dominguez's wife.

Ella: Hey there! What a pleasant surprise. You hike?

Nelly: I've never hiked before so I don't have any equipment or
anything, but I'm down.

Ella: Equipment? Lol. Do you have sneakers and a water bottle?

Nelly: Yes.

Ella: Send me your address. I remember you aren't too far from me.

Can you be ready in an hour?

Nelly: Yes.

ELLA WAS surprised and excited to hear from Nelly. It was merely coincidence, possibly. Ella didn't believe much in coincidences and she had every intention of getting some alone time, but suddenly felt like she could use some company. Because of work and Ryan, she had isolated most of her college friends, and rarely found time to make new ones since. There was definitely a vibe with Nelly and she figured a hike would be a safe place to explore it. Plus she needed to de-stress, and nature was just the thing to help with that.

She ran home to throw on some tights and a pullover. She noticed that Ryan hadn't been back home either, even more reason for her to do her thing and not worry about him.

She arrived at Nelly's a little over an hour later and sent a text letting her know she was there. Nelly came right out as if she was waiting by the door.

Ella couldn't help but laugh as Nelly walked to the car with her all pink from head to toe.

"It's just a hike, not a fitness fashion show." Ella teased as she got in the car.

"Well if you must know, this is one of my very few workout outfits. And it was a gift. And I like I said, I've never been hiking before, so I didn't really know what to wear."

"I'm just teasing. You look cute. And you look fit."

"Looks can be deceiving." She flashed that same look from the night before. They picked up right where they left off.

"So, you've never gone hiking? Where are you from?"

"Queens. Oh, don't get it twisted. I may look like a piece of cotton candy, but underneath all this, is a hardcore gangsta, no lie. And furthermore, I think hiking is some white shit, B." Nelly let her accent come out in full force.

"Ok, ok. I'm scared of you. But hiking isn't 'white shit.' And, what do you do for fun?"

"For fun? I don't know. Take a hot bath, watch my favorite reality shows, and eat junk food when my kids aren't around. Exciting, right?" Ella just smiled. "No, but for real, I don't really have any serious hobbies. I guess I never had any time to figure out what I like to do. Tres and I got together in high school and I got pregnant at seventeen, so I've just been raising my kids since. When Tres isn't playing baseball, he doesn't do much else besides go out with the guys. He comes from a pretty traditional background where they don't believe women should be out and about like that, so I spend a lot of time at home. Pretty boring person I guess."

"You seem interesting enough to me."

"Great! The cool girl thinks I'm interesting." Ella rolled her eyes, and Nelly tried to explain. "I'm just saying you seem to have this adventurous life, with your career and hiking and all that jazz, and yet you think *I'm* interesting." Nelly gave her a look of disbelief.

"Well, I will be the first to tell you, my career isn't as glamorous as it looks. I've just always been the type to feel like I have to push the pedal to the metal in everything and I don't know how to stop. I get that from my dad. But I also spent a lot of time outdoors, my mom was a hippie I guess. They were the most unlikely pair." She sort of paused and smiled picturing them. "Anyway, I hiked a lot for alone time when I was a teenager. It was just a break from the daily for me. It was really the only time I stopped thinking about performing so much and just existed with the moment, the trees and all of nature. Damn, I sound like a hippie too." They both laughed. "I haven't even been in a while, but I realized today that I need to get back doing the things that give me peace. So you hitting me up was right on time to pull me away from work and home for a bit."

"I hear you on that. So where are you from?"

"I'm from everywhere. I'm a military brat so I was born in England and raised in about 7 different places before my dad retired from the military and we moved to Northern California."

"I see you, you're like a Creole gumbo, all light bright and full of a bunch of flavors."

"You got jokes. We will see how much energy you have to laugh after we hike."

"Ok, now you're scaring me. You straight up have me out here in the wild."

"You good shawty." Ella tried her best New York accent. "If you're running around after two kids, then you can make it. We are going up to the Wisdom Tree."

"The Wisdom Tree, huh? I could use some of that in my life."

Ella parked. She put her hand on Nelly's leg. Nelly stiffened with both anxiety and excitement. She had many thoughts running through her mind, all of them landing back on Ella. "Look, not to sound creepy, but I did stalk you on social media and some stuff came up. I'm sure you know what I'm talking about. And you don't have to talk about it. I know you just met me, but I just want you to know that you can if you want."

Tres was the farthest thing from her mind at that point. She softened her muscles and smiled at Ella. "Thanks. To be honest, I barely want to think about any of that. Let's hike!"

Ella grabbed a backpack out of the car that had a built-in water bottle and a mini speaker attached.

"Wow, you're official huh?" Nelly was impressed.

Ella put on a playlist and guided Nelly up the trail. It was as if both of them were transported to another space and time where they had no other obligation but to discover each other. Nelly told Ella a little about her kids, and Ella filled her in a bit on what it was like working with the players. They shared similar struggles despite living in seemingly different worlds; finding time for themselves was a rare occurrence. As they spoke, they both felt their words were landing on eager ears.

When they reached the Wisdom Tree, Ella began to stretch and then instructed Nelly to sit with her and meditate.

"Meditate? Ok, now you really on some white shit."

"Actually, it's some brown shit, Indian to be exact, but my white psychologists did introduce me to it. For me, meditation is just a form of praying. It's just about guiding your thoughts and focusing your mind so you can make better decisions." Ella pulled a small blanket out of her bag. "Here, sit." Nelly sat down with suspicion. "Now close your eyes and pay close attention to your breathing. Observe your heartbeat and think about appreciating your body and your mind for bringing you this far in life."

Nelly started to relax.

Ella continued, "Now, imagine floating or flying or just doing anything where your mind and body are completely free from gravity. Try to picture your younger self standing in front of you. What are her dreams? What are her nightmares?"

Nelly's mind took her to the first night she spent in the group home. She remembered the fear and anger and her eyes began to fill with tears. Her cheeks ached as she held them in and took a deep breath. Ella continued, "Look deep into her eyes and let her know that everything is going to turn out fine." She paused. "Relax your body and breathe into the places where you feel tight. Focus on your present self, right here, right now in front of this Wisdom Tree. Ask for guidance and strength on this journey called life and have faith that every step is necessary in this process." The wind began to blow as if these thoughts were being carried to the One in charge. "Now, just take a few moments to visualize your desires and goals and think about what it is you want right now."

Ella stayed quiet for the next few minutes as she did the same. She judged herself for not making more time to meditate and allowing the tension to get out of hand with Ryan. She promised herself she would do better.

SHE GENTLY BROKE the silence with an audible inhale and exhale. Nelly opened her eyes and took in the view. "Wow, that was actually kind of cool."

"Cool. I told you it wasn't so bad. I'm glad you liked it. Let's make our way down. I feel clearer already."

"Me too!"

The drive back was just as fluid. It was as if they had been best friends since childhood. Neither one was putting on any airs. They were equally delighted to be heard and relieved for the opportunity to share real thoughts out loud, without the fear of judgement. Ella couldn't remember laughing so hard with anyone in a long time. She almost felt silly for thinking sexually of Nelly, realizing that she may have found a good friend in her.

Nelly was enamored, not wanting the time with her to end, and wondering how they could see each other again, soon.

7

Tres was packing for his first road trip with his new team when Nelly got back home. He was leaving that evening for two series, one in Colorado and the other in Washington, a total of seven days. She headed straight to the shower and turned it on. He walked out of the closet.

"Can we talk Nelly?"

"About what?" Nelly undressed, making zero eye contact.

"Anything really. You haven't said much since we got here. I know you said you need some space, but I need to understand what that means. Explicame?"

"No." She got in the shower, unbothered.

"Ok, fuck it Nelly." He instantly regretted his aggressive tone and switched it up. He sat down on a bench by the shower. "I'm really trying here and it seems like you just want to give up. I actually scheduled to go talk to someone you know? And now you've just been out the house and on your phone and I'm just wondering what's up."

"What's up with what Tres? I'm taking some time to clear my mind and figure out what it is that I want. You know, you might find this hard to believe, but I have dreams too. And I hate how you have this timeline for my anger. You think I should be past this already and things should be back to normal. But I didn't even want to come here. And if you feel like you can't give me time and space, I can just go home." She put her face in the water to continue avoiding eye contact.

"This is home now Nelly. Don't talk like that. I'm just saying we can still communicate about day to day stuff."

She turned her back to him, putting her hair in the water.

"Mmmmmmm, you mean I can listen to you tell me about Tre's world? I'll pass. I've had enough of your world for now, which is what I'm telling you. I want to spend some time thinking about what I want. You know I want to do something to express myself like take some kickboxing classes, or paint or I don't know, start a podcast. That's a thing now."

"So you want to start a podcast about what? From a few Communication courses you took a few years ago? I don't think it's as simple as that Nelly, but sure, take some more classes."

Nelly wiped away a circle of steam on the glass shower and looked at Tres directly. "Actually if you remember Tres, the first time we met was when I interviewed you for the school paper. I'm sure that memory is foggy because I never got a good interview since you tried to get at me the entire time. And then, because I missed so many of the meetings hanging with your ass, I eventually got dropped from the newspaper club. So when I took those communication courses, it was to explore a childhood dream of mine. But oh wait, then I got pregnant again so I had to leave school since it wouldn't make sense for you to stay home with the baby. And now the kids are in school and I have the time to maybe explore my hobbies or maybe even start a career." She began to rinse the soap and Tres got up to grab her robe.

"A career? Ok, ok, Nelly. I get it. Women always get to thinking being a wife and a mother ain't enough for them. They have to do something more as if that's not an honorable position in this life. All I'm saying is you doing the best job in the world in being there for our kids with as much as I'm away. And I know it may not seem rewarding now, but one day the kids will know the sacrifices you made to make sure they developed into the people they've become. You know I feel indebted to my mom because of everything she put on hold to be there for me and make sure I was able to follow my dreams."

She turned the shower off and he held the robe open for her to get inside, leaving his hands on her shoulders. She pulled it closed and walked away from him towards the sink. She looked up at him through the mirror.

"Yea, you feel indebted to her because she constantly reminds you of all those sacrifices and how much you owe her because of that. And it seems the more financial trouble your parents get into, the more sacrificial stories she has."

"Wow, Nelly. Tell me how you really feel."

"Whatever. How I *really* feel is not sacrificing my entire existence to cater to the dreams of my children or you. I feel like showing them how to chase their dreams no matter what life presents. What I want them to know is that you don't let a single mother fucker in this world stop you from chasing your dreams, nor do you put them on hold for anyone, not even your kids. I mean men certainly don't."

He softened his tone. "Ok, honestly, I don't even know where all this is coming from. And I'm not trying to upset you. But I'm going to let you do your thing. You have always supported me and I intend to do the same for you. So do you. Start a podcast, start a magazine, hell, become a reporter. Let me know how I can help."

He put on his best smile, got up, and reached in for a kiss. She gave him her cheek. Still, he found some comfort in the fact that she was just looking for an outlet to express herself.

Nelly knew he was offering his support from a place of desperation. But she didn't feel like she needed his blessing for anything. She didn't know where all this talk was coming from either. Her words had been a bit extreme, as she knew that life is sometimes about making sacrifices to allow the growth of others, but at this moment, she was fed up with being on pause for what felt like an eternity. She just knew that at the Wisdom Tree, she pictured herself sitting behind a microphone. It wasn't quite clear the vision she was having, but she intended to find out.

She knew there was one thing she agreed with Tres on, she was going to go after her dreams. With him going away, it provided the opportunity to focus on herself. There was no need to harbor any negativity towards him, she had a plan in mind and she said what she said. Later that evening, she helped Tres finish packing and dropped him off at the stadium. She bought a journal and a few other things on the way home to get organized.

RYAN DROVE himself to the stadium soaked in dread. It was one thing to deal with drama at home where your interactions with the team would be limited to the ballpark. On the road, you were forced to see your teammates to and from the games, on the flights, and coming and going in the hotel lobby. Seven days was a long time to play duck and cover. Even longer when most of the days' insomnia robbed him of sleep. Ryan was a sociable guy by nature, and any behavior other than that would indicate he was struggling. And although most, if not all, the men on that team would understand if he wasn't himself under the circumstances, that would not suffice for Ryan. To make matters worse, his closest friend on the team, Robert Patrick, had just gotten injured and wasn't on the trip.

Ryan sat in his usual seat on the plane and in Robert's absence, one of the pitchers sat by him. The team plane was spacious, composed of only first-class seats, clustered in groups of four, facing each other. Some players slept, some watched movies on their devices, some played cards, laughing and talking shit the entire flight. Ryan was prone to do the latter, but his usual crew was scattered, one of which was a friend of Tres and went to sit by him.

"Hey man, you doing ok?" Rick, the pitcher, was an older guy. He was most likely in his last season and had experienced pretty much the full gamut of what you could in the sport. He knew no matter how Ryan tried to front, that he was feeling his lowest on the inside.

"I'm kosher. Ready to get some much needed rest."

"That's one way to look at it. But you don't have to fake it for me man. I'm not going to press you, just want you to know I'm here if you need to talk."

"Thanks, Rick." They both put on their headphones and Ryan fell asleep right away, thanks to a pill one of the trainers gave him.

THE NEXT MORNING Nelly went to check out some schools for the kids. She didn't know what else to do with her time except to make sure everything was in order for her family. Nelly had mastered 'adulting' long before she became one. She had helped raise her younger sister and ran the home when her mom ran the streets. Now, with resources, Nelly operated their household like a Fortune 500 company. All Tres had to do was focus on securing the bag, a rather easy job compared to Nelly's.

She handled every detail of their affairs, including aspects of Tre's deals and contracts. She made sure he was where he was supposed to be at all times, managed all household and support staff, and even worked hard to keep his familial relationships strong, mostly by doling out money. Even in high school, that's who she was to Tres. She would do his homework, wash his uniforms and cleats, make him ice his sore muscles, and ensure his only focus was baseball. His parents, coaches, managers, and agent could always depend on Nelly to get Tres to do what they needed him to do. Doing all this, of course, didn't leave much time for her. She took pride in how much she was able to handle on the daily, but deep down, she wished she could be applying her skills to something she was passionate about.

After she finished up at the school, she drove down to the beach. She knew she needed to make arrangements for them to get all their stuff moved, but she didn't want Tres to think he was in the clear. She didn't plan on leaving him and breaking up their family, but something needed to give. She couldn't continue in this way. She parked and went to sit on a bench to make a list of things she needed to get done, but thoughts of Ella distracted her, making it impossible to resist the urge to see her again. She waited a while before texting.

Nelly: Hey.

Ella: Hey!

Nelly: I just wanted to say thanks for yesterday. I'm feeling inspired and I had a really good time hanging with you. Hope we can get together again soon.

Ella: How about tonight?

Nelly: I was hoping you say that. What do you have in mind?

Ella: Junk food and reality tv?

Nelly: Lol, you speak my love language.

Ella: 7pm. I will send you my location.

8

"I thought you asked if I wanted to chill."

"I did, why?"

"I mean you look a few degrees above chill." Ella's eyes scanned every inch as Nelly skimmed past her and welcomed herself through the front door. Although Nelly was over-dressed, Ella was appreciating each bit of it from her hair and makeup, down to her heels. In stark comparison, Ella was wearing some lounge clothes with her hair pulled up into a messy bun.

"A few? Hmph." She walked past Ella into the corridor. "You smell fruity."

"Well, I did add some orange oil in with my facial blend."

"Ooooh fancy."

"Oh and I just cut up some fruit. Come in the kitchen. Should I go change?" Ella teased her.

"Stop being silly. You look cute. Don't mind my appearance. I rarely get to get dressed without having to get kids ready so I went all out for the occasion."

"I definitely don't mind." The flirting was effortless.

They walked down the hall shortly before being in the open

kitchen and living area. The kitchen lights were somewhat loud but negated by the dimness of the rest of the huge space. An oversized plush sectional took up a good amount of room and still there were various tables and a few conversation chairs scattered throughout the space. There seemed to be a wall of records, but it was an imposing shelf containing possibly hundreds of albums and books. Nelly instantly walked to skim it.

Ella observed in peace while she sat in one of the stools at the kitchen island and faced Nelly moving her fingertips in no particular fashion across titles and covers, pausing occasionally with quick familiarity.

"Pick something. The record player is right there." She softly broke the silence and pointed to the shelf near the corner bottom, right above some built-in cabinets. Nelly suddenly felt pressured to impress her, but saw a Chaka Khan record and grabbed it with coolness.

Ella had a small charcuterie board set out along with fresh fruit and chocolates and didn't move from the stool. She couldn't see what Nelly selected and waited patiently with a curious smile appearing between bites. Nelly laid the needle in the groove and walked towards the island to sit next to Ella. As she got closer, she put the slightest of rhythm into her steps, just enough to make herself that much cuter. They both started snapping their fingers and bobbing at the same time in the song. They laughed and Nelly picked up a strawberry. She examined for a second before biting into and said, "Is this a setup?"

"What do you mean by that?"

"You said junk food...."

Ella scoffed, "Yea, you don't see these dark chocolate covered pretzels and peanuts?"

"Yea I see it, and I'm now clear on your definition of junk food."

"Well, I wouldn't have minded some chips and sour candy, but I got caught up with work earlier, so I didn't have time to run out. This is the most junk I had in my possession."

Nelly was sampling everything she had set out and seemed pleased. It made Ella think of the munchies.

"You smoke?"

"Smoke what?"

"Ding, ding, ding. I knew it. Follow me. I rolled us a little joint just in case you did. I save these moments for when I'm home alone and need to destress. Ryan's not a fan." Ella got up and started walking.

"I didn't say I do."

"Yes you did. The only people that say 'smoke what' are people who smoke weed." Ella looked back and motioned her without leaving much of an option.

"I don't think that's true." Nelly followed.

They walked out onto a patio that was encased by screens with a retractable roof. Most of the screens were open allowing Nelly to see that the house was situated on a hill and that the level she entered through was the second story. Ella sat down on an outdoor sofa and opened a decorative box sitting on a table. Inside was the joint, a lighter and a matching ashtray.

"I don't know what to make of you." Nelly smiled. "This just keeps getting better."

Ella lit the joint and gently pulled. She leaned her head back and coolly blew out the smoke. Nelly looked out and noticed the views. The yard was articulately decorated with a pool, spa, and other water features. The lush landscaped included fruit trees and a garden. It was a beautiful night with the city lights far enough in the distance to allow the stars and the moon to steal the show. The weather was perfect and every-thing about the indoor/outdoor room was peaceful.

"Let me hit that." Nelly walked towards the couch and reached for the joint.

"Oh, this?" Ella smiled and handed it to her. "You sure you know what you're doing?"

"Girl, bye." Nelly rolled her eyes and drew the joint to her lips. She took a long slow pull and held it for what seemed like too long. She parted her lips and let a cloud of smoke fall out.

"Ok, I see you. Not as square as you said."

"When did I say I was square?" They both laughed and Nelly sat on the sofa perpendicular to Ella. She put her feet up and made herself comfortable and continued smoking.

"Slow down, youngin. Puff, puff, pass. Don't tell me you're too young to know the code. How old are you anyway?"

"Twenty-six. So I ain't no 'youngin' and age can't tell nothing about what one knows."

"Yea, I guess you're right about that."

"And you?"

"Just hit the big 3-0."

"Ok, so you grown, grown." They both laughed, then got quiet. The THC was cruising through their bodies and they took a moment to bask in the feeling.

Nelly gently broke the silence. "You know sometimes how you're coasting along in life and the sea is calm and the sun rises and sets on the horizon most majestically." Nelly closed her eyes and allowed her head to drift. "Maybe it's always that way but for some reason, you're suddenly really noticing. It's like although everything is cool right now, and I should just enjoy it, it's like the beauty and power are overwhelming and I can't help but think about the inevitable storm." Nelly paused, but Ella stayed quiet. She continued, "An ocean is not without waves, right? My greatest struggles take place in the future *and* I'm still holding the struggles of my past. That shit causes friction in the present moment. You know my body and my mind are like in totally different places. I just have to release the energy. It's like I have something trapped in my body, and even though I get moments of relief, that heaviness always returns to its spot in what feels like my womb. Is that weird?"

"You're high."

Nelly smacked her lips and frowned. Her sweetness was almost too much for Ella to bear.

Ella felt guilty. She *was* in fact listening to every word that Nelly was releasing from between her full little lips. And that was the problem; those sweet ass words dripping from those sweet ass lips. She adjusted her gaze and tried a more friendly voice.

"I'm saying you must be lifted because you're speaking my thoughts. We're like intergalactically connected right now."

"Whatever."

"No, for real. You perfectly described what I feel like right now. I mean, I'm experiencing a pretty intense body high, but in my mind, I feel so here, so connected. I have no desire to think about the future. Honestly, I think that sounds more strange now that I'm saying it aloud."

A cool breeze crept onto the patio and Nelly shivered. "So how about that wine?"

"Is that all that you want?" At least that's what Nelly thought she said.

"What?" Nelly asked eagerly.

"Is that what you want?" This time, Nelly's hearing seemed to be snatched back into this world.

"Uh, yea. Sorry." She smirked. "That's what I came to do right?"

"Right. However, I just wanted to offer you some different beverage options since I personally don't drink when I smoke. I can make you some delicious, fruit-infused water, chilled to perfection, my personal recommendation. Or, any other beverage such as coffee or juice?"

"I will go with the chef's recommendation since everything else tasted delectable." They got up and headed inside.

Ella couldn't help but see all of Nelly's softness and imagine what that might taste like.

"What?" Nelly pretended Ella said something, just to let her know she was on the same wavelength.

"Now you're playing. We can sit on the couch. Let me grab the drinks."

Ella poured two glasses and handed one to Nelly. "Tell me what you think?"

Nelly erupted in laughter after her first sip. "I think it's koolaid?"

"Yea, fruit-infused water and I added a bit of organic cane sugar." She winked at Nelly and they walked towards the couch.

Nelly sat down but kept her back erect and slowly rolled her neck. She dropped her chin to her chest and let out a sigh. Now that she was high, she could pinpoint the tension in her body and had a desire to work it out.

"You good?" Ella set her glass on the coffee table and scooted closer to Nelly, placing her hands on her shoulders guiding her back to face her. She started at the base of her skull, rubbed down through her neck working her way down Nelly's arms.

"Oh my gosh, that feels amazing." Nelly breathed deeply. Ella gently lifted Nelly's bra straps and allowed them to fall to either side. She rubbed softly where they had left an imprint in her skin. Her touch was magical, spending time in Nelly's most tender spots.

"I'll be back." Ella got up and walked out of the room. Nelly almost wanted to tantrum as she was just feeling completely relaxed and wondering why the massage ended so abruptly.

Ella was gone for about ten minutes, and just when Nelly was thinking of going to check on her, she returned in a bathing suit and robe, with another bathing suit in hand.

"Come with me."

Nelly got up with curiosity and followed Ella down some floating wood stairs lined with beautiful art pieces. Ella reached back for Nelly's hand. "Watch your steps." The overall space was dark aside from the gentle lights on the stairs illuminating the descent and some modest spotlights that showcased each piece of art. Ella's house was an entire vibe. When they reached the bottom, Ella released her hand and proceeded down yet another long hallway and turned into a large bedroom, that immediately featured an entire wall window with the same view of the city as the patio. Nelly noticed an oversized bed was one of the few objects in the room, but the lights were low and they continued walking until they appeared in a bathroom seemingly just as big as the room. In the center was a huge jacuzzi bath filled with water with smoke quietly escaping into the space. The smell of lemon, eucalyptus, and lavender slowly greeted Nelly's senses. Ella handed the bathing suit to her and pointed towards one of the closed doors. "You can change in there."

Instead Nelly unzipped her skirt right there and had to glide it down and step out of it due to its desire to appear part of her skin. Ella turned and walked towards a wooden and glass door. Nelly removed the rest of her clothing and slipped into the bathing suit.

She walked towards the sauna. "Damn, you are fancy. You got your very own spa."

"When you work as much as I do, you barely even have the time to visit a spa, so it's necessary to have one in my home."

Ella gave her a robe and they went inside. There was music playing low from the speakers in the sauna. Nelly smiled at Ella.

"You feel comfortable?"

"Comfortable? Girl, I feel like I'm in heaven. Your friends must be in love with you."

"I really don't even have time for leisurely company either

these days. But yea, I have a couple close ones that live else-where, and whenever I do get to visit them when I'm in their cities, we try to hit up a bathhouse."

"A bathhouse?"

"It's a Korean spa, kind of like this but on a much larger scale. Lots of pools and rooms with different temperatures and stuff."

"Hmmm." Nelly was curious.

"Maybe we can go one day."

"If it's like this, I want to go soon."

They stayed in the sauna for about ten minutes and then slowly melted into the jacuzzi. The water was hot and they were already full of heat, but Ella had a pitcher of ice water with two glasses and a plate of cucumbers and a bowl of lemons.

"Maybe you should run a spa with the magic you're pulling. You did all this when you left the living room?"

"I usually keep water in here, but I brought all this other stuff before you came because I planned to do this after you left anyway. But when I saw you were tense, I figured you could just join me."

"Well thank you."

"Here, put these on your eyes."

Nelly laid back and did as Ella instructed. She began to wonder why Ella would invite her to do all this. She had insta-stalked Ella as well and even scoured the WAG gossip blogs to see what was up with Ryan. He came back clean and both of their social accounts painted a picture-perfect marriage, a very attractive power couple with no public drama. The few mentions of Ryan were just women saying he won't budge from his wife and that he must be pussy whipped. One line in partic-ular stayed with her, "Beware, his wife is known to put her voodoo on anyone she catches in her web. More women are after her than her man." She wondered if maybe she missed something in what Kim and T were telling her at the charity event about Ella. She wanted to investigate.

"So, is this what you and Ryan like to do?"

Ella seemed unbothered by the question and kept her cucumbers on. "Sometimes. He's not really a bath guy but I convince him to soak his muscles and sometimes have it filled with ice. I think it's important for everyone to try to care for their body in this way."

"I looked you up on social media too. You two are cute together. Perfect little marriage." It was more of an inquiry.

"Yea, we are a power couple I guess you call it." A bit of unease darted through Nelly's eyes. Ella continued, "Marriage is a partnership. And that's what I wish it was called, complete with a partnership agreement and/or contract. It is not a merger. It's a collaboration. It's where two separate entities decide to work together in some aspects of which they can mutually benefit each other in some way facilitating each other's growth. Where people go wrong, is in merging into one. That would require a subtraction of something because one plus one equals two and sometimes three, but never one. Things go wrong in any partnership when there is a belief that one has given up too much of themselves and realizes the other can't make them feel whole. You feel whole by staying whole, and never subtracting from yourself, only adding to the other partner. You collaborate with your partner, but never lose your brand. So in that sense, Ryan and I have a very strong partner-ship. It is not without disagreements but we can move past those after a few days of gathering our thoughts in our own space."

Nelly again felt dissatisfied, she said all that to not say much. She removed the cucumbers from her eyes and sat up.

"Welp, I see why you're a boss in your field. That sounds good, but I'm not quite sure that's how most of the world wishes to operate."

"Maybe not, but that's how I operate. I'm not going to douse my own fire to help someone light theirs. That's counterintuitive. What I will do is build a bigger fire to generate enough heat for others. And hopefully, they throw a couple logs my way when they see mine wearing down. Ryan is the same way, but lately, something has him spending more time in the darkness. And that's ok too because we all have to have a balance between light and dark, but when you start pushing your darkness into my space, it's time to reevaluate some things."

———

ELLA DIDN'T WANT to talk about Ryan anymore and stood up to grab her towel. Although she was in love with Ryan, the feelings for Nelly were creeping like a snake along bubbling tree roots. To say it was an excitement in her gut solely, would be farthest from the truth. Already, it felt so much deeper than that. And this conversation was making her feel uncomfortable. She walked towards another closed door. Behind the door was a closet the size of a guest room. She grabbed two sets of clothes and set one down on a bench near the sauna. "I'm going to rinse off and moisturize. Get out when you're ready. You're free to do the same and you can put these on unless you want to get dolled up."

Nelly took off the bathing suit in the bath, stood up and reached for her robe. Ella had rinsed quickly and left the shower running. Nelly realized why she was hurried when the lukewarm, almost cold water sprinkled on her skin. She did an equally fast rinse and wrapped herself back into the robe. She used the salve that Ella was using from a glass jar. It was like a mixture of shea and coconut oil with a light citrus scent.

She put on the clothes which felt like silk to her skin. "What is this, velvet?" Nelly gave her best Jewish Eddie Murphy impression.

Ella laughed, "Ha! Were you even born when that movie came out?"

"Do people only watch movies from their lifetime?"

"So no you weren't, but I see you, young little old soul." Ella was able to bring the vibe back. "You have to go or you up for some ratchet tv?"

"I'm always up for some ratchet tv."

They walked back through the bedroom out to the hallway towards the stairs. Instead of going up, they went into a room right next to the staircase. It was a media room complete with large recliner chairs and a massive, intricate sound and visual system. Ella grabbed two blankets from a large basket and they sat in the first row.

"This chair and blanket might drag my ass to sleep." Nelly got cozy in her seat.

"It's ok if you fall asleep. It's probably best anyway. It's a little late to be driving on a Friday night."

They put on some ratchet reality tv and shared a few laughs but it wasn't long before slumber kidnapped both of them.

9

Ella woke up in a panic the next morning and noticed the blanket folded on the chair next to her. The house was completely quiet. She walked upstairs to get her phone. She had one missed call from Ryan and several messages related to work. She scrolled and found Nelly.

Nelly: Thanks for last night. I hope you don't mind, I let myself out. I had to let the cleaning lady in at 6. I miss you already.

ELLA DIDN'T KNOW how to respond. She felt the same way, but was trying to process this all in her mind.

Ella: I had fun!

Nelly: Now it's my turn to show you a good time. When are you free next?

Ella: I'll be out of town for a few days for work. How's Saturday night?

Nelly: Yes! Will you pick me up at 8:00?

Ella: Yep, see you then.

THE ENTIRE DAY, Nelly's mind was consumed with thoughts of Ella. She played with herself three or four times just to try to clear the sexual energy from her body and mind, but it was only making it worse. They both wanted to text each other, but were aware there needed to be boundaries. Neither one was one hundred percent sure what was even going on between them, nor sure the other one felt the same. However, they were sure of the tension in between their legs and wished to relieve it.

Nelly decided it was best to move forward with getting things sent to LA. She needed something besides Ella to occupy her mind. She had been ordering things online and decided to start making the house a home and getting the kid's rooms ready for their arrival. They would be joining her in LA in less than a week, and although she was missing them, she was brainstorming how she would juggle her time with Ella with their presence.

ON THE ROAD, Tres was playing his ass off. He hit for a cycle in the first game of the series and hit two home runs in the next two games, helping them win all three. Everyone would've thought he was on cloud nine, but that wasn't the case. That's just who Tres was. He could bury pain and frustration so deep inside, that he could bottle it up and let it explode in a magnificent way. It seemed as if nothing ever bothered him, but the truth was that baseball was like a punching bag. Hitting the ball was his expression of pain and struggle. Making great plays, diving, jumping, throwing hard, that was his way of screaming and shouting. And that worked out well for him.

That's also why he liked aggressive sex. He had to find other women to do that with. Nelly needed tenderness, and he reserved his most delicate self for her only. One of his little side pieces kept hitting him while in Colorado. She knew he was there, but he decided to ignore her the entire time. He intended to wean himself of these women and focus on Nelly and his family, considering he could sense a difference in her. The team was already arranging for him to meet with a psychologist as part of the trade agreement to address the drinking amongst other things. He wanted to use that as an opportunity to seek help for his other issues so he could prove to Nelly how much he wanted to change. He was also thinking about Ryan and felt he could use some mature guidance in the meantime so he hit him up to see if they could grab a bite before the late bus to the field. They hadn't talked much since the night of the charity event, except for small chatter in the locker room and dugout. Tre wanted to connect with Ryan because he looked up to him. He imagined it was difficult to watch someone not only take your place, but come in with a bang and outperform you. He didn't want that to affect the relationship he felt they could have. Ryan agreed to meet him. He knew better than to take anything Tres was doing personally. And to his surprise, he was becoming a fan of Tre, it was hard not to.

"Thanks for meeting me man. How are you?"

"I've been better."

"I bet. Look, Ryan, I appreciate the way you're treating me since I've been here. Guys don't always handle these situations well and it's just opening my eyes to a lot. More so in me manning up in other ways in my life. And I see what type of man you are to your wife, and ya'll don't even have kids. That's admirable, but it lets me know I need to get my shit together and quick. I don't mean to get so personal man, I just need someone to talk to."

"You're good. Not like I have anything else to do right now." They both laughed a little. "What's up? You're killing it out there so I'm guessing your struggle is at home, and understandably so."

"Yea. It's like I only know how to solve my problems with baseball and sex. And with baseball, that's great and it works, but clearly the other, not working out so well. And I'm scared I might just lose my family over it. And if I lose my family man, I will lose baseball too, because they're my why, my motivation, and energy. You know?"

"I do know. But you have to have tunnel vision in this game. Focus only on your family and the game. Just like you said, taking your eyes off those for anything else at all, risks losing them both. It's a lot of distractions out there, for everyone, and a little more so for us because of the spotlight. The more you mature, the less you allow yourself to be distracted by things that offer no value to you, just temporary pleasure that is detrimental in the long run."

"I feel that."

"And I feel your struggle too, Tres. I don't pay much attention to the women, but I've indulged in other vices, pills mainly, you know, that I feel caused me to be in this position right now. Allowing the pills to numb the pain, so I play through it, instead of putting in the time to heal my body from the inside out. Sometimes we all looking for the quick fix. Only in retrospect do you see there isn't one. Nelly's still there, man. That means you can make it right. But it's going to take time, and discipline and healing from the inside. You know we have a good team psychologist, you should see him."

"Already scheduled man. The team set it up, but I plan to take advantage since I have to anyway."

It reminded Ryan that he should probably see the doc too.

He wished he could tell someone what was going on with him. He knew because of who he was, there was a high chance the person wouldn't keep it to themselves even with client confidentiality.

"Do I need to find a new marketing agent? I mean, you might have to let go of everyone except Ryan. He over there letting these rumors get to him." He started laughing. Ella had flown to the Bay Area, mostly to visit Joe Enriquez.

"Boy, please. Ryan ain't thinking about you or anyone else for that matter. He's injured and needs some rest. He knows I'm not checking for you."

"But you would be right?"

"Wrong. You're too cocky for me Joe. I deal with you in exactly the capacity I wish to, by securing the bags with you, so cut it out and stop playing with me."

"I know. You know I'm messing. But for real tho, you got any friends like you? I am ready to choose the lucky one you know, and settle it on down."

"Joe you aren't ready to settle nothing down. You're just getting started and besides, you don't need to be distracted with getting serious with anyone right now. You're hot in your career and we need to capitalize on that."

"See, I knew it. You just don't want me to be with someone."

"You ready to talk business or not?"

"Ok, ok, yes Ella. Business." He put on his fake serious face. " Who else needs Joe Enriques to boost their brand? I can't keep helping these smaller brands, I'm getting too expensive for them."

"Calm down. Those smaller brands are the long game. We choose the right ones and we set you, your grandkids and your great-grandkids up for life. You know Vibe, the pH water." Joe nodded. "I did a deal for Troy Jackson almost five years ago that paid almost nothing upfront, just shares, and equity, and he almost said no because no one, not even me, heard of them at the time. They were a small company that didn't even have an office. You know how fucking happy he is he didn't. He's made enough money to not have to ever get paid in baseball again. Those are deals I hunt for. Now that's not to say they all hit like that, but play a few chips on a few different companies and the chances of one hitting increases." She handed him a flyer. "I'm going to this later. If you have time, come. I want to introduce you to some people. Let you get a feel for yourself. I think there might be some good opportunities for you. And maybe you can find your wife. I have some friends that might come through."

"Now you're talking. I'll be there."

They finished their meal and Ella headed across the bridge to Oakland for her next meeting. She was in her old stomping grounds but needed to make sure her work was done before playing. She invited some friends to a launch party that evening, an easy way to mix business with pleasure. Nelly crossed her mind a few times, but Ella could always busy herself enough to change her focus, especially with work. She spent the next couple of days visiting clients and even made time to stop by Cal and visit her old professors. She and Ryan talked briefly just to check-in, but she knew it was best to just give him space and time. She wanted the week to skip a few days just to get to Saturday.

SATURDAY EVENING, Ella pulled up outside Nelly's and texted her. The door swung open quickly and Ella could hardly contain the shortness of breath at the sight of Nelly. They made eye contact and her sheepish grin made Ella feel drunk. Or maybe she was, because she hadn't eaten much in anticipation of seeing her and took a shot on an empty stomach before leaving the house. Nelly hopped in, leaned over and kissed Ella casually on her cheek. It was awkward yet natural.

"Where are we headed?"

"It's called The Spot. You ever heard of it?"

"I don't think so."

"Here's the address." Nelly leaned closer to show Ella her phone. She had fantasized so much that her impulse was to grab her face and suck on her lips. She restrained. Ella put the address in her phone, and turned on some music for the background.

"So, what did you do all week?"

Besides think about you? Nelly kept those words in her head. "Well, I did a little writing."

"Really? About what? I didn't know you write."

"I mean, I don't really. I mean, occasionally, nothing special. I was always the journaling and poem type when I was a kid. I even wrote for the school paper in middle school and a little in high school before I met Tres. And aside from writing a few poems and jotting down stuff about the kids, I haven't written much in years."

"So, what did you write today?"

"Mostly jotting down some ideas I've been having since the meditation at the hike. Then I smoked, and wrote a little poem." Nelly paused and flashed a bashful look.

"I want to hear, and don't say you don't have it, because I know that's not true."

Nelly pulled her phone out of her purse and cleared her throat softly. Ella turned down the music and smiled.

"You are beautiful and carefree. I love the way you look at me. You find things that nobody sees. And when I catch you staring, you don't look away. You simply smile and continue to look at me that way."

"Wow. So delicate and sweet. Mary Jane is quite the muse."

"Who?"

"Mary Jane." Ella started singing, "I'm in love with Mary Jane, she's my main thing...she makes me feel alright...."

"Oh." Nelly started laughing. "That Mary Jane. Yea, I think that definitely helped."

"And ideas?"

"Oh, just thinking about starting a podcast or vlog or something. I don't know. Just been thinking about when you asked what I like to do and realizing there's a lot I like to do and want to do and maybe I should be doing those things."

"Of course you should! Why aren't you?"

"Honestly, I don't know. Guess I've been focused on the wrong things. And lately, my focus has just been a little different. You know? But thinking about the things I'm thinking about is making me feel really good, so I just feel I should capture that somehow."

"I can dig it. Let me know if you need help with anything. I'm sure I can point you in the right direction depending on what you're trying to do."

"Thanks, Ella. That means a lot." They smiled at each other and Nelly glanced out of the window as the car went from a sprint, then to a jog, to a crawl. "I think this may be it."

After thirty minutes, the map had taken them to a somewhat secluded industrial park. Ella was a little confused, but Nelly was sure they were in the right location. On an otherwise unmarked building, they saw the address written largely above tinted glass doors. "1212." There were cars scattered in the parking lot, and just one person leaving out of the building.

"Well this is it."

"Now you're scaring me. You just moved here. How do you know about this place?"

"An old friend." It was her friend from high school who she had kept in touch with all this time. It was one of the few friends Tres encouraged her to hang with. Tre assumed that the people in the places where they were hanging would have zero interest in Nelly. Mainly because he knew who her friend was back in high school—before the transition from Lawrence to "Laura." Nelly lived vicariously through her friend's adventures and Laura knew Nelly better than her own family did. From the ball scene to the bathhouses, she had exposed her to it all. Laura knew Nelly's deep down affinity for women, for the feminine form in general. She was instrumental in her appreciation of everything about it, and took her into a space where she was adored for some of her deepest insecurities. Nelly was inspired to maintain her self-confidence despite the treatment of a man. That could sometimes seem like an arduous task, but her mother had always taught her the same anyway so she knew what it was supposed to look like.

NELLY OPENED the door to get out, and Ella was able to fully take in her get up. Her sharp black stiletto red bottoms did everything to put her body on a pedestal. A thin silky skirt barely draped under her ass revealing her small shapely figure, and an off-the-shoulder blouse grazed her skin in the same way Ella's tongue imagined. Aside from her appeal, Ella could see that she was comfortable with who she was underneath it all. It was that, more than anything, drawing her in. Ella got out to follow Nelly. She was wishing she hadn't let that liquor get into her.

They walked through the doors into an elegant reception area with a sexy lounge feel. Tall velvet couches lined one wall of the room. Across from the couches was a tall desk with a woman standing behind it, dressed like a fine dining hostess. She looked up from a screen and gave a neutral smile. There were no other people in the room beside them.

"Two?" The only things on the desk were a couple of pens,

the computer and a true desk lamp that barely illuminated a portion of the space as if to keep the darkness captive.

"Yes, please"

"Ninety dollars. Would that be cash or credit?"

Nelly pulled out a bill.

"So...." Nelly looked around as she said this. They were both wondering what next.

"Here's your change. Please enter through the doors right that way. Any questions can be answered there." The woman motioned towards a door. "Enjoy." Her gaze returned to the computer as nonchalant as ever.

Ella went to grab the handle, but the door swung inward with a man standing there gesturing for them to come inside. It was dark with purple and red lights shooting carelessly through the room. Suddenly, silhouettes were everywhere. They could see movement, barely recognizing any facial features in the darkness. The hallway became narrow making it impossible not to skim people's shoulders and arms. Ella grabbed Nelly's hand and switched to lead her in. The feel of her fingertips resting on her skin made her warm. They could see some lighting up ahead and bottles.

Ella realized where they were and led Nelly straight to the bar, eager to calm her nerves. "I don't know what to think of you. This just keeps getting better."

Nelly smiled.

They ordered two double tequila anejo's on the rocks, and headed towards an empty booth in the corner. They scooted in, thighs touching, still holding hands. Nelly let Ella's hand go on her thigh and placed hers on top, indicating to keep it there.

"Cheers."

"To expression."

"To expression."

NELLY SIPPED down her entire drink and bit her lip with eyes full of lust. And as quickly as the drinks went down, the temperature rose. The movement of her legs spoke clearly. The energy of the place combined with pent up desires encouraged them to waste no time. Ella slid her hand between Nelly's thighs, straight to her panties. The material was soft and already wet. She leaned in and grabbed Ella's ear gently with her teeth, "Touch it," she whispered. Ella obliged and allowed their lips to greet. Effortlessly, their tongues licked and rubbed each other. Ella pulled back and looked around for a more secluded place. She pulled Nelly from the booth and walked down one of several small dark hallways. In the hallway were several doors. As one swung open, they caught a quick glimpse of a few people groping and kissing on much larger couches. Although mostly indistinguishable, it seemed to be a fairly mixed crowd. A door to the left opened and appeared to be vacant aside from a couple walking out, one leaning on the other for balancing, laughing and enjoying each other's company. Ella motioned towards the door and as they tried to exchange exit and entrance, one of them fell into Nelly. The other one grabbed him, and looked at the ladies, starting to apologize. They all froze for what seemed like an eternity. It was the left fielder, Robert Patrick. His companion was a young-looking, pretty little thing with a face beat for the gods. "Yaaaaaaas Queens. We need to party with y'all fine asses." Robert steadied him and tugged for him to keep moving. There was no need for the rest of them to exchange words. They instantly vowed secrecy with their eyes. Ella squeezed Robert's hand and they continued in separate directions.

The moment was fleeting yet numbing. The ladies entered the room and just as fast locked the door behind them. Nelly laid back on the closest sofa and pulled Ella on top of her. The tension allowed no inhibitions. Ella slid her hand up Nelly's skirt, maneuvering her body so that she straddled her thigh.

The blood rushed to her head. She moved her hand, fearing that this overwhelming sensation would cause her to orgasm quickly with very little movement. She moved her hands to Nelly's blouse which came up easily and her small breasts were unbridled and waiting anxiously. The evidence of children made her feel even deeper for Nelly's natural beauty. Ella softly caressed them and allowed her tongue to glide over every inch, spending extra time kissing and sucking her nipples. Her skin was melted creamy milk chocolate with delicate caramel lines drawn artistically across her outer thighs to her ass. Nelly grabbed her hand and placed it in her wetness and Ella treated that entire space until she came, squeezing her thighs tightly around her wrist and forearm, and at her climax biting Ella's shoulder. As her teeth sunk it, it was as if Ella was snatched out of a vortex. She suddenly felt sober and scared and reality stood over her like a dark imposing figure.

"You ok?" Nelly put one hand on Ella's cheek, worried about what she was thinking.

"I just need some water." Ella managed her same smile because Nelly's touch felt so good and gentle, but she was trying to process what had transpired since they entered the club. She was always a very calculated person, and this was completely impulsive. She immediately thought of Ryan and how he would be returning the next day.

This wasn't just another random hook up with some random woman that she would never see again. Ella wanted to rush home and sort this thing out in her mind, but she didn't want to alarm Nelly, so they chatted and laughed for a bit, while Ella drank two glasses of water to help dilute her alcohol.

Nelly noticed Ella's phone going off and asked if she was ok again.

"Yea, work stuff. We should get going. You ready?"

"Sure."

As they were walking out, they spotted Robert with his

friend. Ella and Nelly looked at each other and smiled with the same shocking disbelief. Robert caught a glimpse of the ladies and gave a little open-handed goodbye and got in the passenger side seat of his car. They waved back and he sped off, wheels screeching.

They hadn't even reached the car when they noticed police lights and instantly wondered if Robert had gotten pulled over. He didn't seem intoxicated, but they were more concerned about the circumstances. Again they looked at each other, eyes full of worry. Ella drove past the police car and could slightly see that it was Robert's car pulled over towards a ditch on the road.

Ella slowed but knew they weren't supposed to be there either so she kept driving.

"I hope they're ok."

"Me too."

THE OFFICER APPROACHED the car with only the flashlight. He didn't put on the bright police lights and even turned off his headlights. Robert thought it was strange for a pullover in a dark area.

"Well, well, well. If it isn't Ms. Tina. Wow, look at this fancy car. Did you get a promotion? Haven't seen you working your usual area lately." Tina stayed quiet, clearly nervous. "And who do we have here? You going to introduce me to your friend. He looks strangely familiar. But it couldn't be who I think he is. I mean, what would he be doing running around with a gal like you."

Robert knew the officer recognized him but he was still confused about why the two of them were so familiar. His stomach started to turn. He had met her online and this was only their second time hanging out.

"Is there a problem officer?" Robert finally said as calmly as possible.

"Oh, baby. I guess you didn't tell your friend here about your services or did you because that too would be a problem?"

"No, I didn't. She' just a friend. We were just hangin out."

"Really, well what are *you* doing coming out of a place like that?" Now he was speaking directly to Robert. "Man, what are your teammates going to think when they find out you're batting for the other team." He erupted with laughter. Robert caught a whiff of the liquor on his breath, but he kept quiet.

"Did you hear me?"

"Yes, sir." He paused. "Tina is my friend. She called me to come pick her up."

"Really?" He put one hand on his hip and the other one his chin, tilting his head with disbelief. "That's really strange because I've been sitting outside this building for a while and I didn't see you pull up. And I'm sure I would have noticed this beauty." He tapped on the car. "This here vehicle cost more than my house."

"Look, sir. Ihave to get home to my wife. Is there something I can do for you to move this thing along. How about some season tickets, right behind the plate?"

"That sounds nice, but I'm already a holder. How about you fine fellas step out of the car."

"Is that really necessary?"

"I mean, I can call back up if that's going to be an issue."

They both got out and walked to the back of the car.

"Empty your pockets." Robert put his keys and wallet on the trunk and Tina pulled out two lollipops and a condom. "That's all you got sweetie? I doubt that."

The officer walked up behind Robert and told him to put his hands on the car. He shoved his hand in the back of his pants and reached towards his crotch. He came out with a baggie full of goodies; a colorful array of molly, perc, and

Xanax. "Well, what do we have here. I'm going to be famous after this bust. Center fielder Robert Patrick caught with a hooker and drugs." He tilted his fat pink face back and did his same sick laugh.

"I'm just playing. I'm a fan man and you and I seem to have a lot in common." He winked at Tina. I guess I could let this all blow over. All I want is one of those." He looked towards the lollipops sitting on the truck. Tina looked at Robert confused but started to reach for the sucker.

"No, silly. Not those per se. I was speaking figuratively, you know. You know exactly how I let these things *blow* over Tina." The officer walked to the side of the car that put them completely out of view on the dark road.

Tina followed him, but the officer quickly stopped him. "Not you Tina. Why don't we let our new friend do the honors."

The officer unbuckled his belt and unzipped his pants. "Next up, Robert Patrick." It was a sinister announcement. He pulled out his pink, pinky sized penis as Robert walked towards him and knelt to the ground. He felt tears rushing through his temples into the back of his eyes and held them there. If there was a camera on the patrol car, they were positioned out of view. He noticed the ring on the officer's finger and figured this debauchery would never see the light of day—it was the only way to protect his darkness. He closed his eyes and thought about baseball.

———

THE FORTY OR so minute drive back to Nelly's was quiet, except for some music kept super low in the background. The entire evening had been surreal. Mostly, the women were worried about Robert and whether they should've waited to make sure things were ok. His presence in their evening was completely drowning out their own experience.

Ella pulled up to Nelly's house. Nelly lingered for a bit. "Well, that was an interesting evening, to say the least. When can we schedule another playdate? I want to put it on my calendar."

"I'll text you. My work schedule is a bit hectic over the next few days. I have a player that was traded recently and we need to explore his market and strategies for partnerships in his new city. You know, exciting marketing work." Nelly could sense the run-around.

Neither one was sure of a fulfilling departure. But Ella was sure that work was not what she wanted to consume her right now. She shook it off. They were both aware that their husbands would be returning in the morning. Nelly initiated the lean in and they locked lips for a soft kiss. They held there for a moment, both hesitating for the night to end.

Nelly got out of the car and closed the door. She took only a couple of steps before looking back at Ella to wink. In a large group, Nelly's charm would go unnoticed by choice, but alone with Ella, she was in full swag.

* * *

ELLA WAS LEFT ALONE with her thoughts and emotions. She debated calling Ryan. It was late, but she knew he was probably up. He hadn't contacted since he left so she decided against it, figuring she would wait to talk to him when he returned in the morning. When she pulled up to her house, she felt an overwhelming sensation of guilt. She had enjoyed Nelly immensely, but of course, there was an underlying rumble. Everything she and Ryan built together was there in front of her and here she was sorting out her feelings for Nelly in their driveway. She had so many questions. What the fuck just happened? Where would they go from here? What would their interactions look like in the field? Could they just pretend this evening didn't happen and move forward with a friendship? She got out the car and went inside, wanting in some ways to erase the night.

NELLY, on the other hand, was feeling floaty. She felt like a teenager, all giddy. She replayed the sex scene from the night over and over again in her head and felt compelled to write. It was her last night to herself, so she poured herself a drink and sat on the couch with a notebook and pen.

> *Do we ever align in spirit*
> *After the day has taken its toll on us*
> *Such an empty comfort*
> *Despite the fact that we lie under the same stars, it*
> *   isn't nearly close enough*
> *And you know this*
> *You felt my heart*
> *The connection stimulates me*
> *I know for sure I never felt this way about loving*
> *And I can't seem to figure why you have this pull*
> *   on me.*

She grabbed her vibrator for a nightcap and drifted off into a world where only she and Ella existed.

10

Tres returned from his trip to find Nelly in a different mood. He thought this was the last straw for him, but with the kids back, Nelly seemed to be completely back to normal. She even greeted him with a kiss in the morning and made his favorite breakfast. Although an ounce of suspicion sat quietly in his stomach, he knew to keep it there with the hopes that she had simply moved past his immaturity once again.

"Damn, baby, your skin is glowing. What you got another little slugger for me in the oven?"

Nelly smiled and smacked her lips, "Hardly. Just using some new oil on my face. Been doing a lot of self-care over the last week or so."

"Te veo." Tres was feeling good looking around the table at his family still together and coming off some good playing on the road trip. He wanted Nelly to know that he meant what he said. He wanted to be better but he didn't want to dig up any drama.

"Oye amor, I was thinking of taking the kids to the field today to meet some of the guys."

"Yay!" The kids erupted in cheers.

"We have to make sure that's ok with Mami, primero?" He winked at Derek, the oldest.

"Yes, that's fine. Y'all go upstairs and get ready. And please brush those teeth." She had to yell out the last part as they took off running before she could even finish saying yes.

Nelly was standing at the sink and Tres walked up behind her and put his hands on her shoulders and massaged them. An image of Ella shot into her mind, and she quickly dismissed it by putting her hand on one of his with a gentle tap. It wasn't even an act. She felt love for him, as her friend. She was truly unbothered by his actions because her affection towards him in that manner was completely dissolved. It had happened almost overnight. She was remembering who she was and what she had to offer the world. This new sense of confidence didn't leave much room for pain and for her to be dwelling on someone who was drowning in their insecurities.

"Thanks for breakfast baby. It was delicious as always. You coming to the game?" He knew that question was a stretch.

"Not today. I will send Maria to look after the kids. I have some stuff I want to work on here at the house." He assumed she was talking about unpacking.

"Ok, text me if you want me to bring you food after."

Nelly was in her own universe. She was already planning to text Ella to see if she wanted to meet up. She wondered if this was the same feeling Tres had with his extra-marital activities. If so, she could understand why he couldn't stop. The excitement was like a drug.

ACROSS TOWN, the Smith household was a different story. Ella was taking extreme measures to comfort Ryan in an effort to reduce her overwhelming guilt. Unlike Tres, he wasn't receptive. Every effort she made to ease his tension was only creating more division.

"Ryan, I'm really worried about you. I get going through little hitting slumps and whatnot, but it just seems that you always get a little withdrawn around this time in the season every year." She was hoping she could prompt him.

"This same time Ella? Have you been keeping a journal about it or something? I go through ups and downs throughout every season of course." A bit of worry darted through his thoughts. Had someone contacted her or had she seen something? He always knew this day would come and he tried many times to come clean and just couldn't find the words. His heart began to race a little. "You know Ella, just forget it. I've told you what the issue is, but you want it to be everything else but that. So until you start by asking yourself, how you're making me feel, then this conversation isn't going to go anywhere."

"Ok Ryan, how am I making you feel?" She tried to sound genuine.

"Now you're just being facetious."

"Actually, I'm not. I'm genuinely asking. Am I making you feel insecure about something? I know you've mentioned the time with my clients quite a bit lately."

"No."

"Am I making you feel obsolete?"

"No."

She decided to get right to it.

"Well, I'm clearly making you feel like you can't talk to me since you're leaving me to read your mind."

He could tell by her tone, she knew something. He suddenly realized that she had been pretty calm the entire conversation and fear raced through his entire body. His heartbeat quickened and his mouth got dry. Here was his chance. He would have to say something anyway as it could very soon be apparent.

The words were trapped in his throat and he could not bring himself to formulate them into sound. "Fuck this, I'm going to the field." He got up abruptly and stormed out of the room. His behavior was borderline crazy. Ella tried to remain calm, but these outbursts were ridiculous, and up until the other night, she didn't deserve to be on the receiving end of his tantrums.

The truth was she did know what was bothering him. If it hadn't been for her own little secret, she might have come out and said it this time.

Years back when news of their engagement was in the media, a woman had reached out to Ella. She told her about their child, a little girl, and let her know right away that she didn't want anything but to inform her from one woman to another of something she might want to know about the man she planned to marry. She said, if she knew any better, Ryan probably didn't tell her and probably didn't plan on it considering the deal she signed prevented anyone from ever finding out. She had receipts so there wasn't even a reason to ask Ryan. She figured she would wait for him to tell her. Turns out, the woman was right. He never told her. And being the businesswoman she was, Ella kept that shit in her back pocket like a piece of lint. She was fox enough to know a get out of jail free card could come in handy one day.

Ella had done the math and knew that his daughter was on the brink of turning eighteen. She figured the girl was able to contact him once an adult. This was by far the most agitated she had ever seen him, and while a part of her wanted to help him work through it, she couldn't help the level of resentment she felt by his omission for all these years. The fact that he wouldn't take his opportunity to just tell her encouraged Ella to start justifying her indiscretions.

Ella: Hey
Nelly: Hi! I was just thinking about you.

Ella: Want to grab coffee?
Nelly: No wonder I was thinking of you, we are on the same wavelength. I'm
at Drip right now. Come on!

ELLA WALKED into the coffee shop and spotted Nelly . She was the brightest thing in the room. She had already ordered for Ella and had her laptop and notebook out.

"What's all this?"

"My creative juices. It's like the floodgates opened and I've just been writing so much."

"That's great." Ella was happy for her but there was a sense of discomfort emanating from her.

Nelly could sense it. "Look, what happened the other night, I know that was pretty crazy."

"Yea."

"But, we can just forget about it if you want. I mean I really enjoy your company. It's just that you know after the time we spent at your house, I couldn't stop thinking about you. Well, to be honest, I've been attracted to you since I saw you the first night at the charity event. I'm in a different space though right now. You and Ryan have a good thing, I know that, and I don't want to be the one messing that up."

"I'm a grown woman. We both did what we did, and I won't lie and say I didn't enjoy it. It definitely caught me off guard and I'm having some trouble really comprehending what's going on."

"Nothing's going on. Just two women getting to know each other, building a friendship. We can leave it at that." Nelly hoped she sounded convincing, and changed the subject, "Can you download this app? It's called Planner?" The app icon was a hand with bedazzled nails. It looked like an app for salon appointments.

"What is it?"

"It's just a messaging app that's a little more discreet and you can send files. I want to be able to share some of these ideas with you on a more private platform. Look." Nelly got up and moved to sit next to Ella on the other side of the table. Their skin grazed each other and heightened them both. Nelly continued, "Here you can basically choose your icon that disguises it as another type of app, that others wouldn't be interested in."

Ella knew where this was headed, but didn't object. In her head, she said "fuck it" too. If Ryan wanted to deal with stuff on his own and make it seem like she was the one to blame, then she would just worry about herself.

"So you want to tell me about some of these ideas?" They remained seated on the same side of the table, and left their outer thighs touching, the most intimacy they could enjoy in that moment. Nelly pulled her laptop from across the table.

"I want to start a podcast. Like, I want it to be a guide for player's wives. You know like a sort of roadmap for dealing with the ins and outs of this lifestyle. I may be young, but I've been through some shit. And sometimes I feel like the women are putting on airs pretending like everything is picture perfect and everyone wanting to seem like their situation is better than the next when it would help for us to be real and support each other. Because of Tres and his public shenanigans, I always feel isolated from the other wives. It's usually the girlfriends and groupies that treat me the nicest, but we know what that is. It's like the women don't want their husbands hanging with Tres as if some of theirs aren't doing the same things. Anyway, I'm not trying to focus on all the negativity, but rather offer ways to keep your sanity and explore ways that we can help heal each other."

"I think that's perfect. Turning a negative into a positive. What have you done so far to organize this idea?"

"Well, I started by ordering the equipment of course. That was the easy part. Now I'm just trying to brainstorm and outline the topics. I at least want to have the first six planned out before I start. I've already been thinking of special guests."

"Do you have a name for the podcast?"

"The Player's Wives Handbook."

"I love it. I see what you did there." Ella was impressed. "I think you're off to a great start and you should continue planning the way you are until you think you're ready to record the first podcast. At that time, we can discuss marketing strategies if you want, you know, depending on your audience and all that good stuff. These days people want to hear the drama and the dirt, and honestly, it's what captures short attention spans. So you have to master mixing in the message with the messy. You know?"

"Yep, well the message is sometimes in the messy."

"I know that's right." They tapped their coffees together to cheers to that.

11

Ryan stopped at a drive-through liquor store and got a bottle of Crown. He pulled over in the parking lot and began drinking right out of the bottle. It didn't take long before he was feeling buzzed. He picked up his phone to change the music and opened Instagram instead. He went straight to Rachael's page. He scrolled back through the pictures of Leila's 18th birthday celebration. He had already seen the pictures a few weeks back and had been trying not to check her page ever since. As the alcohol crawled through his veins, he began to see himself there in the pictures, standing proudly next to his daughter, shining his same white, ear to ear smile that so many, except her, had come to know and love. As he swerved slowly away from sobriety and towards inebriation, his emotions ran amuck, from laughing to crying, to deep levels of resentment that he still held towards his parents for not ever even asking him what he wanted back then. Sure he was scared about bringing a child in the world at only fifteen, but he didn't think it was the worst thing he could've done, and secretly he was a little excited about having something or someone rather love him for who he really was and not his athleticism. But his parents, and their attorneys, his coach, and his "advisor", made it very clear that he would have nothing else to do with Rachel or the child because the situation was being "handled." And by handled he assumed she had an abortion or gave the baby up for adoption. His parents changed his number, forced her to change hers, and even managed to get an order of protection against her.

Even though he was feeling tipsy, he drove to the stadium and went straight to the weight room. There were a few guys in there, including Tres. Ryan almost walked out but didn't. He felt aggressive and a need to throw weight to let it out. He headed to a bench where Robert was stretching, preparing to lift. He started loading up the bar and motioned towards Robert to come spot to him. Robert's nerves went from zero to one hundred, but he managed to play it cool. Tres could see from across the room that Ryan was upset, so there was no reason to leave his workout partner to go talk to him.

"What's up brotha?" Ryan's forceful exhales throwing up the weight inundated the area with the smell of liquor right into Robert's nose.

"Damn, man. You ok?" Robert asked.

"Yea, why?" Ryan was being short.

"You seem upset, that's all." Robert was always ready to play stupid under every circumstance that could potentially be an attempt to expose him. He kept his voice calm.

"Just restless I guess, you know having all this strength and speed, and not really getting to use it. You know?" Robert let out a silent sigh, relieved that it wasn't about him being seen with his little friend the other night. "Well, no you don't know, Robert. You white boys get to play every day if you want, and we over here just as dispensable and unwanted as it was in the 1870s."

"I get it, Ryan so don't give me no lecture. You don't see me all up Tre's face trying to be his best friend."

"What's that supposed to mean?" He stopped lifting and sat up.

"I'm just saying, you coming in here real hot. It's not a good look man. Maybe you should head over to the resort. Get a massage and hit the steam room. Let it out that way man. Trust me." Robert reached out his hand to say goodbye, an extra hint that it was time for Ryan to leave. Throwing up the heavy weights combined with Robert's calm delivery in the background was just what Ryan needed to gather his senses. He placed his hand in Robert's and pulled in for a half hug, tap on the back. Robert was right, he shouldn't have been in there drunk and he appreciated Robert's friendly way of getting him together quick.

He grabbed his bag and headed back out. "It's all good, I soon be back," he said right before taking one last glance towards Tres and exiting the room. He smiled with the arrogance of his early twenties, a time when he convinced everyone he was the man, and all the attention in the world distracted him from what was lurking down beneath his surface.

RYAN DIDN'T RETURN HOME until later that evening. Ella was already in the bed with the lights out, but barely sleeping. She heard him come in and remained still. He went straight to the bathroom and turned on the shower. He came out and crawled in the bed almost an hour later yet still the smell of alcohol pervaded the air around him. Almost abruptly, he moved right up behind her and placed his body strongly up against hers, using his arm to pull her even closer. She could feel his erection and her entire body tensed up. Without scaling back his level of aggression, he did attempt to rub her shoulders, trying to force her to relax. This only made Ella more resistant. She tried to softly take a deep breath as she knew his demeanor could only escalate at this point, being he was drunk and still angry. Ryan didn't offer much effort in the way of softening her before just pulling down her pants and panties and entering her without much success at first. He pulled back, sat up and turned her completely on her stomach, pressing his hand on the back of her neck. She heard him spit and knew there would be no stopping him at this point without further provoking him to aggressiveness. She closed her eyes and reached her hands under her to put pressure on her clit. She thought of Nelly and within minutes, Ryan fell to her side, breathing heavily and snoring shortly thereafter.

The next morning he woke as if nothing had transpired the evening before or for the last few weeks .

"We're still on for tonight, right?" He paused to see if Ella remembered.

She had been distracted from several work obligations lately, but he chalked that up to his treatment of her. He knew he was fucking with her. Unfortunately, it was purposeful. His strategy to avoid exposure of his dirt was to make her feel some kind of way, and the demotion only helped his cause because it gave him even more of an excuse. He wanted to tell Ella. He wanted to reach out to Rachael, his daughter's mom, and inquire about whether his daughter wanted to contact him now that she was eighteen. He wanted Ella to be by his side as he did all this. He was in disbelief and even disappointed that he hadn't told her yet. He never intended to wait this long, but his fear of Ella's disapproval always overpowered his desire to come clean to her.

His pause was enough to jog Ella's memory, as she had seen the notification that they were scheduled to have dinner with one of Ryan's closest friends, also her client, and his wife. His team was in town and they had planned over a month ago for his wife to come on that road trip and meet for dinner. It was not something she could reschedule, but she found some relief in being forced to be amicable with Ryan since he would never allude to anything being wrong in front of his friend.

"No, nothing's changed. I'll get a driver to the game so we can ride together after."

ELLA ARRIVED at the stadium a little early to meet up with Veronica, Dalton's wife. She rarely stayed for a full game so she preferred to do her mingling once it started. She kept wondering if Nelly would be there, and how she would interact with her. She took a couple of shots before she left the house to calm her nerves. She parked in the family lot and took her time greeting the various people she knew. Then she went to the family room to grab a quick bite where she ran into Nelly. It caught her a bit off guard, but Nelly walked right up and hugged her. Nelly's entire body felt soft and warm and inviting. Ella tried not to linger in the embrace, but she was in dire need of Nelly's tenderness. Neither one had informed the other of going to the game so they were both pleasantly surprised. With their breasts touching, the reminder of evenings of nipple to nipple contact struck them both. They pulled apart, but not without notice by some of the other wives. Nelly caught a glimpse of them staring and for a second thought about how she might have to hit them up for some damage control.

Ella and Nelly remained for some small chat before Dalton's wife, Veronica came looking for Ella. Veronica approached them and for a quick second, Nelly was completely thrown off. A wave of jealousy swept through her body realizing she was there with Ella.

"Nelly, this is Veronica Austin, Dalton Austin's wife. Ryan and Dalton go way back and Dalton is one of my clients." Nelly felt silly but still possessive. Not only was Veronica beautiful, but she seemed touchy with Ella. She couldn't help but recall the things she read about Ella, and what the other wives were saying and it suddenly hit her how easily they had hooked up. She began wondering if she was just another wife or woman that Ella was mingling with. Maybe she and Ryan did have some weird sort of partnership or open swinger type deal.

"Hi, very nice to meet you." She watched Veronica closely.

"You guys just got traded here, right?"

"Yes. We've only been here for a couple of weeks now. I like it. I'm lucky to have found Ella. She's definitely made the transition easier." She flashed a little smile towards Ella and moved closer to her as to lay her claim.

Veronica was oblivious but Ella could feel the heat. "Well, we are going to get to our seats. You and Tres are more than welcome to join us for dinner after."

"Thank you, but we have the kids and we have to be up early for some school interviews." Nelly did want to go, only to be with Ella and keep an eye on Veronica, but she knew herself and knew she didn't want to see Ella around Ryan nor did she want Tres around when she was near Ella. It was hard enough to hide how she felt about her in the stadium, let alone in public.

When Ella got back to her seat, she couldn't stop thinking about Nelly. She was completely turned on by Nelly's appearance and even more so at the slight possessiveness she displayed out in the open.

Ella texted her on the app.

Ella: Meet me by the family room.

Nelly: Ok.

WHEN THEY BOTH reached the family room, Ella motioned for Nelly to come with her and they walked around the tunnel to an area far away from everything else. "I want to show you around this place." Ella smiled suspiciously and bit her lip, gazing straight into Nelly's eyes to let her know what she was thinking. She didn't say anything else until they had dipped off down a hallway in an area off of the tunnel that circled the stadium. She opened a door and guided Nelly in. "This used to be the daycare before they remodeled." Before she could even finish, Nelly turned around and wrapped her hands tenderly around Ella's neck and head and they began kissing. Ella lifted her bag over her head in one swift movement and sunk completely into Nelly. It was like water into sand. They fell back onto a sofa in the room. Simultaneously, they reached into each other's panties. Even with raging energy, they managed to stroke each other lightly. With just the right touch, they both managed to climax as fast as masturbation. They were equally impressed at the quick satisfaction. Something about the mental stimulation or maybe that they were rehearsing the scenario in their private sessions so much that it was effortless to please each other. They both wanted the same thing yet, neither one could pinpoint exactly what that was. The feeling felt familiar, and yet so distant.

Luckily, there was a restroom in the area and they were both able to gather their lives back together and return to the game.

They walked back towards the seats and when they got to the family area, Nelly's kids ran up to her and wrapped their arms around her "Mom, we came looking for you. We're hungry."

"Where's Maria?"

"She's getting us some food, she said to go wait in the family room."

Ella stood there smiling.

"Derek and Davida, this is my friend Ella. Her husband plays on Papi's team. His name is Ryan Smith. Say hi, please?"

"Hi." They both replied. "It's nice to meet you." Derek reached out his hand as the more outgoing one.

"Well, aren't you quite the gentleman? You play ball like your dad?"

"Yep. I'm going to play in the MLB too. I'm eight and she's seven." They were both wearing their dad's jersey and looked like exact carbon copies of Tres and Nelly. Derek had the looks and charisma of his dad and Davida was just as coy as her mom. Ella didn't know what else to say. She was absolutely fascinated to see Nelly in that role, and even went as far as to imagine herself as a mom at that moment, yet she felt somewhat awkward knowing what had just transpired ten minutes prior.

"Well, I'm going to get back to my seat. My friend is waiting for me. I'll be seeing you guys around." They both smiled.

"Ok, see you later." Nelly gently squeezed Ella's arm, not wanting to say goodbye.

Nelly had a smirk on her face that Ella swore would give their secret away. She smiled back and hurried back to her seat, checking to see if anyone was paying attention to them. She decided right at that moment she would make very few appearances at the stadium and maybe opt to travel with Ryan on some of the road trips instead. She instantly regretted her lustful behavior and tried to remember if there were cameras in that back section of the stadium. She hadn't even thought of it before when she was horny and thinking about Nelly. This behavior was unlike Ella and she instantly began to criticize her actions. She would have to cut Nelly off. Or at least let her know that they were just friends and that was the last time they would be intimate. She was losing control and it was terrifying and exciting all at once; a feeling she was not used to.

Her actions were not based on emotions. She learned at an early age to see everything as transactional and her psyche held tight to this coping strategy—a skill she developed from her instability as a child. Anytime she tried to veer from this and develop love for other people, her dad would get reassigned and move her across the world. It was tough, but her dad taught her to be tougher.

The game was in the 5th inning when Ella got back to her seats. She asked Veronica if she was ready to head out and grab a couple of drinks at the restaurant and order the food for the men before they got there. She couldn't bear the thoughts she was having for a minute longer. She didn't even look in Nelly's direction on her way out. And Nelly tried not to watch her walk away.

She understood that Ella was struggling but she had no intention of letting up. She hadn't experienced a connection like this since she first got with Tres and even that was different. This was so many things combined into one. In Ella, she saw her childhood dreams that had long been deferred somewhere along her journey. Ella was a dream. She represented everything Nelly was too scared to be in real life. Nelly's mother was the only other hustling business-like woman she had ever truly known and she thought her mom was lonely as a result of it. In fact, her mom had told her that. She wondered if Ella was lonely too. Ella reminded her of her mom, the type of woman her mom would've been had she been offered the same opportunities as Ella.

AT DINNER, Ella presented herself the same way as always; a woman that has it completely together, for whom success comes naturally as a result of her charming nature. Too bad that wasn't the truth. Ella was indeed the actress. She learned to fit into any group under any circumstances, a skill passed down from her father that enabled her to slip into environments bigger than her pond and make it seem like she came from the ocean. She genuinely believed in herself, that she could do anything and be anybody. But that was the problem. She often wondered if she was really doing what she wanted to be doing, or just trying to be impressive to everyone. She had spent almost an entire lifetime trying to be what others wanted her to be, that she was unsure of what she truly wanted and who she truly was. She thought back to the night at the house when her and Nelly hung out. She felt so free that it made her paranoid. That night birthed euphoric sensations that brought her to a time early in her life. She wanted to believe it was the weed but she knew the truth sat right in front of her. Nelly made her want to throw off the chains and it terrified her.

"And for you, Ella, another glass?" Veronica asked as she poured herself another glass of Riesling. She was enjoying every second of her time with Ella. It was difficult for anyone not to. Ella could always make people feel exactly how she wanted them to. It was her gift and her curse. Even though they sat together for two hours, it didn't seem to be enough one on one time when the men arrived. Ryan came right in, sat in the seat next to Ella, scooted close and put his arm around her chair. Ella was impressed at his acting skills and thought maybe they could be up for an Oscar for best duo. She played right into her part of the wife everyone thought she was and they were all smiles the entire meal.

Even though she had committed to ending things with Nelly, effective immediately, it took all her strength not to check her phone to see if she had hit her up. Towards the end of dinner, she excused herself to the bathroom, so she could check her phone. She scrolled through her messages to Nelly's thread. Nothing. She was convinced that she was tripping and this further confirmed that she needed to leave the situation alone.

The car ride home was awkward. She checked the app that Nelly had shown her once more and still nothing. It made her wonder what Nelly was even doing. It was late she realized and began to think she was probably just asleep, but then again, what if she wasn't? *What if she was up with Tres, having sex with him?* Those thoughts made her uncomfortable. When she and Ryan got to the house, he walked straight in and poured himself a drink.

"I'll have what you're having." Ella slipped her shoes off and sat feet up, into a corner of the couch. She wanted to put herself in the most relaxing position possible and continue to pretend that she and Ryan were on good terms. It felt good at dinner, even if it was all an act. Ryan poured her one and plopped down on the couch next to her. She knew what was coming.

"Look Ella, I haven't been in a good place lately, obviously. I wanted to stay strong and not let the team's change affect me. My body actually needs the rest, but that don't make it easy on the ego."

Ella pretended to understand. He continued, "I know I haven't been being the best to you and I'm sorry for that. You don't deserve it. You've done nothing but support me and encourage me."

She tried to stop him. "I get it baby, there's no need to talk about that right now."

"I know. I just want you to know I love you and I know you have my back more than anyone. I appreciate that."

"Well thank you. Thank you for saying that." She looked at him with a graceful forced smile and didn't say anything else.

She dare not let herself get excited about the prospect of him coming clean. She had heard this speech over a thousand times, and it was never followed up by the truth.

Ryan's heart started to beat harder and he thought with the few drinks in him, he could just tell her. He put his hand on her leg and gave it a gentle squeeze and then laid his head in her lap. She rubbed it gently, realizing this wouldn't be the moment of truth after all. All she wanted was to get her phone and text Nelly, but instead dozed off right there on the couch, with

Ryan's head in her lap. Her only option was to see Nelly in the alternate world, her dreams.

JUST A FEW MILES AWAY, Nelly was thinking of Ella while intertwined with Tres. This was the first time she had been intimate with him in months and he was surprised at the intensity. The passion made Tres feel something he hadn't felt in a long time. He was falling in love with Nelly all over again. There was hope. He believed God was on his side since he had made the decision to be a new man. Maybe Nelly could feel the change in him already. For Nelly, the sex was a strange, yet exhilarating experience. Although she was with Tre, she only thought of Ella. Even in the act, images of Ella aroused her and she could see and feel Ella unable to feel the difference between her current reality and fantasy. She moved her body on top of Tres in ways that were unfamiliar to her and led her to climax, collapsing onto his chest shortly afterward. Tres held her, whispering sweet nothings and praying over her and their family softly in her ear as thoughts of Ella rocked her to sleep.

WHEN ELLA WOKE, she was on the couch by herself. She got right up to check her phone, but still nothing. She even checked to see if the app needed an update desperately hoping it was her phone. She contemplated writing her, but started working instead. She had been falling behind on things and needed to regain her focus. Maybe her behavior at the stadium was clear and she wouldn't have to say anything to Nelly to end things. This was better.

Even though Ryan was being a dick, she would try to be there for him. He wasn't the only one with secrets from the past. Nothing she had was as serious as him having a child, but deep down she understood the magnitude of his ordeal and why he would hesitate to share with her.

It really didn't matter what she tried to do or think about, thoughts of Nelly inundated her mind. Every thirty minutes or so she checked the app, refreshing the page to make sure a message wasn't missed. She checked Nelly's Instagram page for any clue to see what she was up to but to no avail. Nelly didn't post anything. Nelly's silence drove her mad. She tried to create any distraction from the longing she felt yet every thought frustrated her. She even considered confronting Ryan with her long held information instead to free him from his conscience. But she knew how much men hate to be backed into a corner and didn't want to further provoke him to lash out. She checked her phone again and when no new messages were unread she flung her phone across the couch.

"FUCK."

TRES HAD BEEN OCCUPYING Nelly's time. Anytime he wasn't at the field, he was going all out being the family man, planning fun things for the kids and surprise dates for her. Nelly watched as he made his efforts to save his family. To her, he seemed desperate and she began to pity him. The more attempts Tres made, the more Nelly wanted Ella. She thought of Ella constantly, but she understood why Ella was hesitant. Her conscience wasn't the clearest either. She knew Tres was thinking things were great between them, and while she wasn't bothered by him, she wasn't enamored by him either. She enjoyed the time he was spending with the kids, but she just wanted to make sure no one was getting suspicious, especially the other wives. She decided to hit them up and attend a brunch they invited her to. Turned out, they weren't so terrible in that environment. However, they did try to ask her questions about Ella. She played dumb and managed to evade their nosiness. She had every intention to see Ella again, but she knew she needed to play her cards right. Nelly knew Ella was feeling the same, yet she wasn't hitting her up either so she decided to make her sweat a bit.

It was over a week before Nelly finally reached out. She had expected to run into her at the stadium, but Ella had been ghost. The team finally went back on the road, and with Tres out of her hair, and the kids settling into school, it was the perfect time to reconnect.

Nelly: Miss me yet?

ELLA SMILED when she saw the notification from Planner. She had just arrived back in LA after spending the week traveling, visiting clients and closing deals. She had timed it to get back when Ryan was leaving in the hopes that she could see Nelly. She had occupied her time for long enough and did miss Nelly. Instead of replying back, she went to meet a colleague for a drink. She couldn't appear thirsty, so she waited until the next day. And so the game playing commenced.

Ella woke up early but waited several hours to text back.

Ella: Yep. Want to hike?

NELLY SMIRKED when she heard the ringtone she assigned for Planner. She had been waiting, but by now, she was starting to figure Ella out and knew she wouldn't reply immediately the day before. Now, time was of the essence with the guys on a short trip.

Nelly: Yep

Ella: You free now? Want me to pick you up?
Nelly: Yes, please.

Nelly has just returned from dropping the kids off at school. She had on workout clothes in anticipation of hearing from Ella. In the time since the hike, she had invested in a wardrobe of athletic wear. She found it to not only be flattering, but comfortable and wanted to be ready at short notice should Ella beckon. Ella was already dressed too and pulled up to Nelly's not too long after.

Ella: Here
Nelly: Come in.

ELLA WALKED UP to the house and Nelly opened the door. She gave Nelly a quick and friendly hug and looked around. It was a large open space, that contained mostly boxes and a few pieces of furniture the night she and Ryan were there. Now, it was fully furnished and grandiose with the many different areas in view. From the door, the living room, game room, kitchen, family room, and full bar were all visible. Natural light poured in from massive windows and an entire wall of sliding glass doors. The interior neutral whites and greys were just the background for all the colors popping in the accents and art. It was very New York: fresh, funky, and loud. Nelly gestured for Ella to have a seat on a couch in the living room. She sat next to her on the small couch, despite several options. A coffee table in the middle of the square of seating had a pitcher of water and two glasses. This was clearly Nelly's area. She had her laptop and notebooks sprawled about and next to one cushy chair a small record player with headphones and a handful of records. Ella looked at Nelly and smiled when she saw that.

"So, is this what has kept you so busy?" Ella hoped that was the only reason.

"Yep, between unpacking and helping the kids get acclimated with school. It's been a little bit of a struggle. Derek can go anywhere, walk right in and make friends. It's not as easy for Davida."

"Yea, I noticed that about them. They're adorable, and well-mannered. Just the kind of kids I would want."

Nelly smiled at the thought of the four of them hanging out. She wondered what Ella would be like as a parent. She was thoughtful and caring, but didn't seem motherly.

"Are they at school now?"

"Yea, they'll be there late today. It's their long day. Language classes and then sports. Maria, my nanny, is going to pick them up. I had planned to meet up with Talia, you know, head of The Hive," she said with air quotes.

"Talia, huh?" Ella raised an eyebrow and slightly threw her head back as if Nelly was joking.

"She had to reschedule, thankfully. But she's not so bad, you know, and I was just trying to make some other friends on the team since you were avoiding me."

"I wasn't avoiding you." She tried to say it with confidence.

"Ok." Nelly shrugged and continued. "Well my kids made friends with hers at the stadium and then she kept bugging about getting together. I figured it wouldn't hurt to try to be cordial." Ella sat quiet, tucking in her bottom lip and slowly nodding as if she was unbothered. But, she didn't want Nelly hanging with the other wives. Aside from their irrelevant ramblings and constant drama, they did possess the ability to stumble upon some true dirt from the mouths of their husbands and they wasted no time shoveling it into an open ear. She had concerns over what they might tell Nelly and Ella wanted to be in control of what anyone knew about her, especially Nelly.

"You don't have to explain yourself to me." Ella looked away from Nelly towards some family photos on the wall.

"So you missed me, huh?" Nelly could tell Ella was putting on airs and wanted to bring her attention back.

Ella did turn right back to her. "Yea, I did. But more importantly, I was a little worried about you. I only went to one game in the beginning of the week, but I didn't see you then and you never hit me up until yesterday. You've been ok? How's the podcast coming along?"

Nelly was irritated at the way Ella made the conversation sound so friendly and professional as if nothing else was running through her mind. She played along.

"I've been good, haven't had much time to work on the podcast, but

I've been outlining all my ideas whenever I get a chance. I just try to keep my notebook with me. You must've gone to the one game I didn't. Anyway, I was just giving you some space. You seemed, I don't know the right word...regretful, I guess."

"I'm having mixed emotions about this situation. But I won't lie and

say you aren't consuming my mind." She paused and Nelly remained quiet, hoping she would continue. " Yet, that's kind of what bothers me. I don't really know why I feel this way. I mean, not that you aren't wonderful and attractive, easy to talk to, fun to hang out with and all that. It's just that I'm really used to being consumed with only work. Like truly, that does it for me, because I feel pretty exhausted outside of my clients. And just in this short amount of time that we have been hanging out, I got fired by a player that said I was neglecting him. So, in a way, I did feel I needed to pull in the reins and get my shit together, but at the same time, it made me realize that maybe I do have too much on my plate as far as work is concerned. I didn't get to spend nearly as much time with you as I would've liked, and even that was too much as far as my clients were concerned."

"Damn, sorry about you getting fired. I'm not trying to interrupt your grind."

"You're not. In retrospect, it was a good thing. Freed me up a bit, and got me to thinking. It's not like I can't afford to scale back, so just trying to figure out why I feel like I have to immerse myself so much. Like, what am I avoiding, you know?"

"Yea, I feel that way too. Not that I have a career like you, but I kind of feel like I do raising a family. It's like I pour so much of me into everyone else's dreams, so I have an excuse why I don't fail at chasing my own."

"You know, I haven't had *these* types of feelings in so long. So this all feels new for me."

Nelly didn't know if she could believe her. "So you haven't ever been with a woman before?"

"I have, mostly before Ryan. And an occasional hook up throughout the years, but just sex and no intimate relationships." Ella was shocked at her own level of candor.

"Does Ryan know?"

"Somewhat. I mean, he's been involved in some of the hook-ups and a couple of times, I hooked up with those women outside of him. I'm pretty sure he knows, but it's nothing we really discuss." Ella kept shifting her legs and clearing her throat. This level of vulnerability made her want to get up and run.

"I don't mean to interrogate you. It's just that I'm definitely feeling some kind of way about you and I don't really know what that means either. All I know is that I want to be around you all the time. I think about you constantly and when I'm with you, I feel inspired and at peace."

"You ever been with a woman before?" Ella felt that Nelly talked with way too much ease regarding all of this.

"There was this one time." She paused in remembrance. "Remember my friend I told you about, Laura, who used to be Lawrence? He, well she rather, used to take me out to these gay bars and every once in awhile there would be a woman I was attracted to, but that was as far as it went. Except a few years ago. I was taking a couple of courses at a community college and I started to crush on one of my professors there. Well, apparently she picked up on it, or was feeling the same and asked to see me in her office after class one day. She came onto me, and although it was something I think I wanted, a picture of her family in the office threw me off and reminded me of my own. Tres was just as reckless at the time, causing me headaches, but, even then, the guilt was too much to bear for me. I quit school that day and never went back. Tres just assumed I was overwhelmed trying to go back to school with the kids still being so young." Again, she paused thinking back to that moment. "Anyway, that was the closest I ever came to being with a woman."

"That's interesting. I've always been attracted to whomever, male or female, whatever race, I don't know. I'm drawn to people's energy, not so much the artificial social representations. If that makes sense." Ella had relaxed her body on the couch, feeling comfortable. Nelly sat facing her, one leg up on the couch, leaning her head on her hand on the top of the sofa.

"It does actually. To be honest, I feel like even as a kid I felt that way. I remember having this childhood friend who I loved so deeply. I used to have dreams about marrying her. I would picture her in a suit in the dream and everything." She chuckled at her own silliness. "My young mind only accepted that marriage had to look like the couple on top of the wedding cake. Followed by babies, a boy and a girl, in that order of course,. And that image that I had is what manifested, with Tres. And it was like it was set in stone for me. My mom was like 'that's the guy you marry if you're smart Nelly'. But don't get me wrong, I was checking for him. Shit, every girl was. And just to command that top spot as 'his girl' felt so damn good." She smiled at that memory. "Until it didn't. But before that, Tres was the best thing in my life, even at his worst. He helped me escape from a bad situation and even let me bring my sister with me. I've always felt like I owe him for that."

"Yea, but for how long? You obviously supported him through his entire career, which means you helped get him where he's at. And you gave him two beautiful children, a boy and a girl. I'd say you paid your debt." They laughed.

"Yea, I don't know. What about you and Ryan? Is it really as Barbie and Ken as it looks?"

Ella scoffed. "Yea right. Is that how it looks?"

Nelly sucked her teeth, "Oh please, you know that's how it looks and you're not going to make me believe it's not intentional, Mrs. Marketing Guru, Boss Queen of Image and Branding."

"Wow, let me write that down. I might need to change my business cards. That sounds catchy." Nelly smiled and nodded in agreement. Both of them were happy to be back in each other's presence, where conversation was effortless and truths crawled out of hiding.

"But really tho, is Ryan the prince charming he appears to be?"

"Honey, there are no real prince charming's. Everything is perception and everything is what you make it. I'm sure you know that. I mean Tres may seem to everyone to be this narcissistic womanizer who only thinks of himself. But is he that bad?"

"Honestly, no. Aside from his little rendezvous, he truly is my best friend. His flaws, I understand them. Because I've been there as they developed and got to see directly what fed into them. I know his pain and his struggles. And not as excuses for his behavior either. I just know my own struggles and how I want those I love to be compassionate towards them. I've kind of always found men to be pretty intimidating, you know, since I happened to have too many bad interactions with them as a young girl. And the way I tried to recover from that was even more detrimental. Tres was the first guy I had been around that was actually very tender and sensitive, behind closed doors. In fact, the way he touched was what I imagined it to be like with a woman. It made it easy for me to trust him, that, and he always was brutally honest with me. He never denied any hookups, even back in high school. He would even go so far as to tell me first sometimes. I've just always felt safe with him, you know, I felt able to be flawed and to have these internal battles. However, I did think he would grow out of it, and that doesn't appear to be the case. And right now, I just feel I'm growing in a different direction. You know?"

Ella had been listening intently. She was intrigued by the way Nelly held so much space for a person's shortcomings, but even more so in the way she articulated herself. Ella had always prided herself in her gift of gab, but she relied heavily on a combination of meaningless statistics and bullshit. Nelly, on the other hand, spoke directly from the soul as if she had lived many lives, much longer than this current one. She was authentic and unafraid to feel the things most people avoided. Ella wished she could experience that level of vulnerability and still be perceived as strong. Unfortunately, Ella navigated daily through male dominance and the slightest sign of forbidden emotions would be deemed as weak. The cold and hard shell she built around herself was suffocating her and she wanted nothing more than to shed it and feel even her own softness.

"Yea, I do know."

"Well you still didn't answer my question about Ryan. But you don't have to. I don't want you to blow your cover." She winked at Ella, and Ella wanted to tell her everything, but she didn't even know how or where to begin. She decided she had given her more than enough for now. An idea popped into Ella's mind, initiating a change of plans.

"You ever been to Dockweiler?"

"No, what's that?"

"It's a beach with a bunch of fire pits. I feel like a campfire and some
smores is just what I need. You already scheduled the nanny, might as well make use of it."

"True, let me grab my jacket and a couple of blankets."

They ran by the store before heading over to the beach. They grabbed some wood, stuff for smores, a bottle of wine, and a few other snacks. They were like young teenage girls, setting out on an exciting adventure.

WHEN THEY ARRIVED, the sun was still stretching above the horizon, preparing for its dip into the ocean. They had their pick of fire pits on the nearly empty beach and chose one closest to the car. It had been a cooler day, and would be a chilly evening. Ella decided to get the fire started so they could relax as the sun set. Nelly laid out one of the blankets, got everything organized, and poured two glasses of wine. She watched Ella as she got the fire going. Her soul felt good, relaxed. She admired the way Ella made spontaneous plans and knew everything needed for perfection. She was a quick thinker, always on her toes, able to please instantaneously. Ella looked at Nelly watching her, waiting with two wine glasses in hand. She fell in right beside her, taking the wine glass from her and kissed her cheek. Nelly felt like a schoolgirl, on a first date with her crush.

"This is perfect." Nelly leaned into Ella and placed her legs across hers. Ella used her free hand to hold Nelly's legs there. Nelly wrapped the other blanket around them and they both stared out towards the sea. By this time, the sun had touched it's toe to the water, beginning its descent into the other world. "This isn't real, is it?" Nelly questioned with a hint of sadness in her voice. There was this little piece of intuition floating quietly in the bottom of her stomach, faintly whispering to her soul. She did her best to ignore it.

"It is right now." Ella leaned back after the sun disappeared beneath the line. She pulled Nelly to lay her head on her and Nelly threw her legs across Ella's body. Ella guided her fingertips across Nelly's face and hair, lulling her into a blissful relaxation. They lay in silence and waited for the moon to make its entrance.

12

After the night at the beach, it became more difficult for Nelly and Ella to see each other, especially when their husbands were in town. Although Ella intended to scale back with work, realistically, she wasn't able to. Getting fired was bad for business, and she knew maintaining her reputation was part of her branding. Yet to scale back, she needed help.She spent time looking for an assistant, hoping that she would also find a partner to take on some of her deals. Relinquishing some of the control would be a huge step for Ella, but she felt it was time. She wanted time for herself, which also meant time for Nelly.

THE TEAM WAS PLAYING WELL, making Tres increasingly popular. On social media, he went above and beyond declaring his love and support for Nelly, in turn making her more recognizable. He flaunted her around as his most prized possession, ignoring every tempting bait that slid his way. Yet, his attempts seemed to marvel the wrong audience. Nelly remained unimpressed, not swayed by his grand gestures- something he wasn't used to. He could sense something was different about her, but couldn't put his finger on it so he stayed under her, trying to implement the strategies he was learning during his counseling sessions. He vowed to work twice as hard to ensure they were ok.

Even Ryan had returned to his normal behavior. Lately, he had a little more action on the field due to the injury of another teammate. The increased playtime helped him regain his confidence. But what helped the most was therapy. He started seeing the team psychiatrist, and although he didn't disclose his secret, their conversations led him to gain the courage to reach out to his child's mother. He figured once he made contact with his daughter, it would leave him no choice but to bring it to Ella. It was time she knew. She had been so patient with him always, even during his worst tantrums. But he knew he would have to do something drastic to get it out rather than anticipating the doom of either Rachael or Laila contacting him, or Ella even.

He sent Rachael a direct message and asked if they could talk. She wrote him back saying she had been waiting for this day for a long time and gave him her number. He was surprised at her quick and seemingly friendly reply. He was headed to step out of the clubhouse to call when he bumped into Robert.

"Hey Robert, you have a minute?" He stood extra close to him and somewhat whispered, speaking quickly and looking around to see if anyone was within ear shot. His furrowed brow was inundated with concern which made Robert nervous.

"Sure, what's up man?" Robert felt his heart rate increase. His conscience was a lion, waiting in the brush. He often thought about the day that beast would make itself known. He found himself nervous anytime someone approached him with a serious tone wanting to talk, assuming that it was a moment he would be confronted about his undercover lifestyle, a secret he couldn't afford to come to light. He tried to smoothly take some deep breaths and appear relaxed, bracing himself for the confrontation.

"I just wanted to apologize about that day in the weight room and thank you. That whole situation could have really gone left for me."

"Yea, no problem brotha. You know I don't want to see you in no mess." He felt relieved, somewhat.

"Yea." Ryan paused, wondering if he could confide in Robert. They had been close since he joined the team, but they never really talked about anything too deep, except for the painkillers. But that was no secret. A lot of the players struggled with pills, especially after an injury. "You know, I really don't get close to a lot of guys, but you've been a good friend to me. And I just want you to know that I'm here for you, and I got your back." The anxiety jumped right back into Robert's body. "You know you could talk to me man, about anything, if you needed to."

"Yea, Ryan, I know that. Same here."

"Good, because I've got something heavy on my heart lately." Robert swallowed hard and darted his eyes to make sure no one was walking up.

He tried his best to remain calm, but here was the moment he dreaded for more than half his life. Ryan continued, "You ever have something happen that you didn't feel like you could tell your wife. You know, besides stepping out?"

"Yea, like when I spend too much money on hoes at the strip club." He laughed nervously, trying to kick his macho, misogynistic act into gear. Ryan smiled, but returned back to serious.

"Like, do you think there are some things better left unsaid?"

"I don't know, maybe. I mean I kinda feel like, if you love someone, there are certain things you don't tell them, especially if you know it will hurt them." His voice started to relax, but he was just outright confused at this point.

"Yea, that's what I'm thinking. But women, they always talking about, 'Just tell me the truth and I could handle it better,' or 'I just want honesty. I just don't want to look dumb, being the last to know.' That shit ain't true."

"For real. They flip out regardless if you not standing at attention twenty-four seven, ready to take orders."

"Word." With that, they dabbed it up. "Well anyway, how's the hand? Any word when you coming back?"

Robert's entire soul let out an internal sigh of relief. "I'm feeling much better, but I guess I have to get another MRI to confirm that things are good. Like you said, "I be back soon."

"You a fool, man." Ryan walked down the tunnel to a quiet area. That conversation didn't help any, but since he had already made up his mind, he called Rachael. The conversation was brief and it was if time had dissolved any anger and resentment that she would have been holding. They discussed planning a meeting for all of them, including Ella. He gave no indication that Ella wasn't aware, only said he would get back to her after figuring out their schedules.

"Ella, we need to talk." Ryan was sitting in the front room when Ella walked through the door. He sat at the edge of a chaise lounge, knees spread, with elbows resting on them, and hands clasped just beneath his chin. It was as if his extremities were there only to prevent his head from hanging low in shame. She sat down across from him. She had news too, but it would need to wait. She realized this was the real moment she had been waiting for all these years because her heart was beating just as fast as his. He looked right into her eyes, "There is no easy way to say this, so I'm just going to come out and say it." He dropped his head and took a deep breath, looking back up at Ella, who was waiting in anticipation. " I have a daughter. She's eighteen." He made sure the last part came out quickly as not to alarm her in thinking he cheated. Ella swallowed hard and nodded, hoping she looked somewhat shocked, but her typical calm self. She sat down on a sofa across from him, saying nothing. He continued, "It was a situation back in high school. My parents didn't think it would be good for my career so they had the girl's mother sign an agreement. It was a terrible thing to do, and even more terrible for me never to tell you." His eyes began to well up with tears.

"Wow." She said with an exhale, possibly her first one since he had begun talking. "I mean, I understand. It's a mistake from your past that clearly has haunted you all these years. That's torture enough. I guess I'm just wondering why you never felt you could tell me."

He could see her processing the same way she did when she ran into public relation disasters with her clients. Even in the most complicated of matters, Ella remained poised and level-headed, instantly thinking up various courses of action. He was just relieved she didn't give a look of disgust and disappointment, that he expected.

"Ella, from the time I met you, I never wanted to let you down. I had never met a woman so confident and in charge, that I felt like I always had to top that. It's like I feel in competition with you. A woman like you needs a strong and secure man, and that's what I try to be. But the truth is that this secret has always made me feel like less of a man for turning my back on my responsibilities. I should've never let it happen."

"But you were just a kid Ryan."

"Yea, but I was man enough to make the baby. I should've figured out a way. And I've never wanted you to know that I wasn't man enough to fix it. I didn't want to disappoint you." In a weird way, he felt somewhat let down by her reaction. He wasn't a client, he was her husband, and wouldn't even the strongest of hearts lose their composure in a situation like this?

"I'm more disappointed that you didn't come to me and let me help you fix it. But I get it." She went over to sit next to him. She felt completely different than she ever imagined she would feel once he said it. In a way, it did make him look weak to her, but she liked it. She grabbed his hand. "What are we going to do about it now?"

"I reached out to her mother. Her name is Rachael. My daughter's name is Laila. They've agreed to meet with us."

"Us? You sure about that?"

"Of course baby. I need you there with me. I feel like at least the only thing I have going for me is that I haven't had any other children. So hopefully she can feel some relief that I didn't choose to raise another child and not her."

"Yea, that's true."

"And even though I want to make things right, I want it to be at your comfort level, Ella. That's important to me."

"I support you Ryan and I think you should make it right. Do what you have to, just please, talk to me, about everything."

"I will. I love you, Ella. I wish I would've told you sooner."

She had a few confessions too, but this wasn't the time. She just wanted to bask in this moment of closeness she felt with him. For the first time, in a long time, she felt connected to him — her husband.

13

Nelly didn't hear from Ella for a few days and was getting antsy. She had constructed a plan to get away for the weekend using her mother as an excuse. As twisted as it seemed, it was the perfect opportunity. Nelly's mother had been battling cancer for about two years. It was well managed and the doctors were optimistic about her recovery, but her weakest moments were during chemo treatments and different family members would go care for her during those times. Nelly would sometimes fly out right before treatment to make sure her mom had every comfort imaginable to help survive a couple of intolerable weeks. She'd hire cleaners to sanitize the apartment, fill the fridge and pantry with produce and healthy means, buy some magazines, and dark chocolate and make sure she set a catalog of shows for her to watch. Nelly knew that her aunt would be there for this round of chemo, and wanted to make sure they were both set up nicely. Tres would never question Nelly going to care for her mother, especially under these circumstances. He was happy to let Nelly access whatever she needed to make this easier for her mother. With this being her mother's third or fourth treatment, she already had everything she needed on deck and could essentially handle any arrangements from home. But it was a good time to have some one-on-one time with her mother even if she was gypping her a day and a half. She made sure to call ahead for everything and set up payments so she could take her to the spa to pamper her first. It was a convenient situation for Nelly who was mostly consumed with ways to see Ella.

Nelly: *Ella, write me back. Can you get away this weekend? I have some exciting news.*

She didn't really have exciting news, not yet. She had set up an entire room to serve as her studio, complete with the equipment she needed to produce a podcast. She had spent most of her time meticulously designing every element of inspiration in the space, her way of occupying her time while simultaneously procrastinating doing the actual recording. She wanted some time with her muse but when she didn't hear back, she decided to force herself to at least do play around with the mic and the software. She sat down at her desk and put on the Lemonade album. She pulled out a cute pipe that Ella gave her from an even cuter jewelry box that was hidden in a compartment in one of her desk drawers. It was always freshly packed to make it quick and easy to take a inspirational, uplifting hit of sativa. She took two slow drags and sat in stillness for a few minutes. Reaching for her pen and notebook, she opened it and wrote 'The Prelude' in big letters at the top of a paper. She let the music seep to her soul, and the words lined up down her throat. She leaned into the mic, and clicked record. The words took their time, coming out cool, calm, and collected as if they had been rehearsing for years.

"HELLO AND WELCOME to the Player's Wives Handbook, this is your comprehensive guide in navigating life as a player's wife. I am your host, Nelly. And please, let me be the first to say I'm no expert on being a wife because there's no one way to be in this world, not as a wife, woman, human, species, anything. This is just a space for voices that can, when used in harmony, offer a feeling of support and love that we could all use in this world and, when by themselves, possess their own unique sound to be acknowledged and respected.

My husband has now played for three different teams, obviously in three different cities. I've met so many types of people, each with their own story, their own blueprint in this existence. Whether aware or not, I gathered a small piece from each of them in our interactions. I've tried to find qualities I like and figure out what I can learn. This isn't always easy ladies, don't get me wrong. I know we can be catty. And some people are closed off to others, which makes it difficult to connect. But I also know that when a group of women do get together to see and route each other on, there is a magic conjured up as powerful as the moon.

Basically, what I'm trying to say is women need to gather, we need to connect, exchange, and uplift each other by sharing our experiences and genuinely offering well wishes and encouragement to see each other thrive. What we all know is, that in this world, being a woman can be a beautiful struggle. These days, I see way too many instances of women tearing each other down and fighting amongst each other. That's completely ass-backward and we must do better.

This podcast is for us to take what we need in order to grow, and to give a nugget for someone else. This is a space of understanding, where we work through our own prejudices and judgements through listening. We create space in us to allow compassion for others.

I started this podcast because, somewhere along the way, I allowed my own voice to get buried deep beneath expectations, preconceived notions, conformity to societal pressures and every other bullshit excuse of not facing and fighting my own demons. Shit, I even lost my own ever-loving mind, somewhere in the past or future, I can't be for certain. But, Frederick Douglas was right when he said, 'Without struggle, there is no progress.' And some of the pain and struggle I've dealt with has not only brought me to my knees, but it has been made public, which left me no choice but to pick myself up and hold my head high. I've managed to listen a lot over the years, and not always by choice. And while I am always here to listen, this is also about me being heard.

My husband's latest rendezvous with an 'Influencer' was a game-changer for me. I finally gave up, threw the towel in, and called it quits. And no, that doesn't mean I left him. It means I've given up on acting like I want something he truly can't provide. Because of that, I've decided to define what we have according to us and our specific situation. It is time to focus on the good, and not be held captive to society's definition of marriage. I know right now this all might sound unconventional, and maybe confusing for some, but that's why we have at least twelve episodes to talk about what this means.

I've dealt with public humiliation, tons of scrutiny and I allowed it to bring me to some of my lowest moments. But somewhere along the way, I got so deep in the darkness that I began to see color there. You know, when we feel like we lost happiness we chase it everywhere outside of ourselves. But when you get desperate and tired, you won't even have the energy to look beyond yourself. Pain takes you to depths of your mind where happiness can only scratch the surface. It is there, that you see all of the lights and the truth. I'm excited to share with you what I've learned on this journey, and I'm hoping it can help someone else.

So once again, this is the Player's Wives Handbook, a guide with tidbits from different perspectives that can potentially guide you along your way, or maybe just inspiring you to keep going.

Either way, I'm wishing all lots of peace, love, and light.

Stay tuned."

With that, Nelly pressed the red square to end the recording and sat back in her chair. She took a deep breath in and on the exhale, made an audible sound out. It was like the weight of a boulder was lifted off her chest. She pictured herself as a bird, finally escaping the cage in which Ella opened for her. She smiled, grabbing her phone to see if she wrote back.

ON THE OTHER END, it was as if Ella opened the cage door for Nelly, but then entered in herself. Ella was experiencing an opposite epiphany. What if existing within the confines was in fact better? Ella had always been a free bird, or so she thought, and it didn't lead to any less suffering in this world. She felt conflicted, overwhelmed. She didn't know how to respond to Nelly's text. She was curious about her exciting news but knew that it was time to have a serious talk with her. Ryan's confession had her in a different space and she had news to share herself. She responded to the text about almost an hour later, around the same time Nelly finished recording. Despite her hesitation, they arranged to meet in Palm Springs at a resort. Nelly planned for them to spend the night after attending an underground party. They could hang out all the next day and then Nelly would fly to see her mother that evening, getting back to LA on Tuesday. Just the idea of it all made Ella forget about what she needed and allow her mind to get excited for the moment. Ryan could wait. She had waited all these years to come clean to her so she would take her time and do things the way she wanted, which included getting to see Nelly in an intimate way one last time, before letting her know they should just be friends. In her head, this would all go over just fine, although it would be hard. For now, she needed to organize her schedule in a way that wouldn't arouse any suspicions in Ryan.

―――――――

THAT FRIDAY, Nelly had Tres drop her off at the airport and then rented a car to drive to Palm Springs. She arrived early, hours before Ella would be there. She hung out in the room for a while before showering and getting dressed for her evening. She wanted everything to be perfect, including the way she looked. She took her time to paint her face naturally and then slipped into a long maxi dress that hugged around her small curves. She figured she would head to the bar to take the edge off the anxiety she felt about the podcast. The feeling was so confusing; an excitement that made her stomachache. She thought back to what her mom had always told her, "Nervousness is just the excitement of growing pains. You have to go through pain, no matter how big or small, in order to grow." She knew, without a doubt, that this was just the thing to free her. She had to confront her fears, seek to understand them, and then defeat them. This process would take time, probably forever. But it was necessary if she desired to remain here.

Nelly had been in the bar almost two hours, slowly sipping through her drinks, toggling between people watching and scrolling through her phone. She checked the app anxious for Ella to arrive.

"Hey Nelly." Nelly turned at the sound of her name and held in a gasp. "We haven't quite had a formal introduction," Robert greeted, moving his hand towards hers. Nelly extended her hand and glanced around looking for Ella with confusion.

Javier, a friend of Tres, sat nearby in the restaurant booth when he heard Robert's voice. He watched as he conversed with the woman in a form fitting red maxi dress. He had seen the woman earlier but hadn't realized it was Nelly until this moment. He made sure not to be seen and took out his phone to text Tres.

———

"I'm guessing Ella didn't tell you I was coming. I asked her if we could meet up and she said she only had about an hour available if I was willing to drive way out here. So here I am. Is she here?"

"Not yet. She should be any minute. Want a drink?"

He sat in the chair next to her. "So, how are you liking LA so far?"

"It's all that I imagined it would be and then some." They chuckled in agreement.

Ella walked up behind them. "You guys started the party without me?" She looked to see if anyone was with Robert. "You here by yourself?"

"Yea just wanted to talk. Can we grab a table?"

"Sure."

They headed over to a quiet area and Robert sat across from them. "Do you mind Nelly being here? I know you said it was about business."

"No, it's perfect actually. I just said it was about business, but really I wanted to talk about that night I bumped into you guys."

"Oh...okay...." Ella said unsure of what he had prepared to say.

"I just wanted to apologize first and foremost for putting both of you in an awkward position. I know it makes it super awkward to have witnessed me with another woman, well what I thought was another woman, and then have to be around my wife." They tried to keep their facial expressions unchanged, but couldn't help the slightest rise of an eyebrow, and almost unnoticeable tilt of the head. "And I'm not saying I'm innocent, but I definitely didn't engage in any -"

"Robert, it's fine," Ella said interrupting him. "We are just as guilty. We were there together."

"Like together, together." Nelly chimed in and snuggled up to Ella. She felt this was her opportunity to share her feelings with someone, anyone and it felt good.

"Oh...ok, I was kind of wondering about that. I didn't really know what that place was, so I was kind of thrown off by the entire evening. I'm guessing both your husbands don't know, but your secret is safe with me. I was just hoping ya'll could keep it on the low too that you saw me there."

"No one is in a position to disclose anything, agreed?"

"Agreed." They said in unison.

They had a few more drinks with him and Robert headed out shortly after. Both Nelly and Ella understood he wasn't ready to admit who he was or what he liked, and they weren't there to drag him out of the closet. They were aware of the complexities of a man in his position and how devastating that information could be not only to him, but everyone around him. He had a wife, kids, and a prominent position in a professional sport that was not willing to face the reality of several men in his exact predicament.

"So, you said you had some exciting news?" Ella asked after Robert was out of sight.

"I started the podcast." Nelly burst out laughing. "I literally just pressed record, started talking, and then published it online." She paused, realizing the enormity of what she did. "I've never felt so... so...." The tears welled up in her eyes and she looked at Ella. Ella's face was full of concern, and then with a teary smile, she said, "Free."

Nelly grabbed Ella's hand. "And you, you helped loosen me."

"Really?" Ella said shyly. "And all this time, I thought I was the one following you down the rabbit hole."

"You unleashed me." Nelly moved in to press her lips into Ella's. She pulled back when she realized where they were. Let's head out. I want you to meet Laura, she's meeting us there. I will tell you about it on the drive."

THE GPS TOOK them thirty minutes north at what seemed to be a residential or resort clubhouse. On the inside, there was a front desk receptionist, and two separate entrances on either side, distinguished by male and female signs but with patrons going in wherever. The lighting was dimmed with candles and a multitude of plug-in lightings that flashed different colors. Laura was waiting in the lobby. She embraced Nelly and gave her a kiss on each cheek, then grabbed Ella's hand and directed her to turn full circle.

"My, my, my, girlfriend. You've done well." Laura cut her eyes to Nelly and then kissed Ella's hand. "You are stunning baby. You two together deserve it all." Ella blushed and threw a few compliments back. "Well don't waste no time huntys. Time is money in here, literally. Go enjoy yourself. I will be on the other side, creating a scene. Let's do brunch tomorrow so I can get a full dose of Ms. Ella Darling."

They hugged and went separate ways after paying the entrance fee. There were designated male and female sides, although not strictly enforced. Once on the other side, they walked to the area for personal belongings. Individual lockers contained a robe, two towels, slippers, and a small baggie with gummies and peppermints. The smell of lemon and lavender filled the entire place. There were multiple smaller pools with varying temperatures displayed, a few open showers, a steam room, and a sauna. As more people came in, they could tell this wasn't the first event of this kind for many. Some started the party in the initial showers, lathering each other up, while others were doing the same as Nelly and Ella, simply enjoying the luxuries of the facilities with someone special. The music reverberating softly created the perfect vibe and before long Ella and Nelly were indulging completely.

"Could it be that all my dreams and fantasies have come true. I mean, baths, music, edibles, saunas, and love all in one moment." Ella felt the same and almost fixed her lips to say it, but instead closed her eyes to let it all sink in. They hung out for about three hours before someone arranged a ride back to their room for the night.

* * *

HOURS EARLIER AND MILES AWAY, Tres had received the text from Javier.

Javier: Hey man, I'm over here at Blue. Nelly's here with Robert I think. You said she left town this morning, todo bien?

Tres: Naw man, everything is cool. Nelly must have a twin. I took her to the airport this morning.

* * *

THE NEXT TEXT was a picture of Nelly and Robert standing at the bar.

Tres was startled by her appearance. She was wearing a dress he hadn't seen before. He couldn't recall the last time she wore something this sexy for him. Yet, now he could not erase the image out of his head.

Although they weren't lip locked, everything about their language shouted that there was something between the two.

He knew that look. She used to give it him. It was the same look that made him decide at only nineteen that he was going to marry her and be with her for the rest of his life. He would save her and protect her from the world. Tres felt a pit open across his entire stomach and threw the phone to the passenger seat. He pulled in the next parking lot he saw and tried to breathe deep. His chest was tightening as were other muscles in his body. He felt his heart beat accelerate and started to panic, thinking he was having a heart attack. Just then, someone knocked on his car window. He jumped, startled by the sound.

"Hey Tres, sorry to bother you. Would you mind signing this for my son? He really looks up to you man, " the fan asked.

Tres let out a nervous laugh, as he realized that he wasn't dying from a heart attack. The pain in his chest was caused by the picture of Nelly with Robert. He remembered back to the last time he felt hurt like that. He was only nine when he walked in on his mother and his dad's best friend kissing. Both his mother and the friend tried to convince him of what he saw, and he could see the fear in their eyes. He imagined how his dad might feel and decided to never speak of it again. It was the first, but not the last time he witnessed betrayal in that way, but figured it was all bigger than what he understood since he saw a lot of adults, especially his father, engaging in that behavior. Ever since then, he used anything to make sure he didn't feel that way, alcohol, pills, weed, attention.

He signed the magazine, smiled, and then rolled up the window and drove off. The image of Nelly in the picture resurfaced and the pain returned. He pulled over again and called an old friend. After a short exchange he called Nelly. When he didn't get an answer he waited a few moments and tried again. He called Nelly repeatedly, but her phone kept going to voicemail. He even tried her mom, but there was no answer. It was late on the east coast so he figured she was sleep. About thirty minutes later his friend arrived.

"Hey, Tres." The woman got into his car. "I haven't heard from you in a minute. You said you wanted to numb some pain?" She pulled a small plastic bag from her purse and grabbed two pills.

"What is it?"

"Something to numb the pain."

Tres snatched the bag from her and gave her a wad of cash.

"Whoa, slow down killer. You can have them, but don't take more than two. Those are really strong, even for a stud like you." She leaned in and grabbed his dick through his jeans. She was surprised to find it soft which was never the case when he called her. "Oh you stressed, stressed. What, did your wife finally leave your ass?"

"Yo, get the fuck out."

"Damn, Tres, I was just playing. You are bugging out. You should let me help you relieve some of that tension." She tried to grab his face to pull him towards her.

She tried to grab his face but Tres turned his head and looked out his window. "I said get out."

"Suit yourself. I hope you're in a better mood next time you call me. I miss you." She blew him a kiss and closed the door.

Tres thought about telling her to come back and let her blow him but instead, he took four pills out the bag and swallowed them.

ELLA SAT up and quietly left the bed. She hadn't slept much in the few hours they had been in the room. She looked back at Nelly sleeping peacefully and her stomach turned at the thought of placing a detour on Nelly's newfound path. She deserved to know sooner than later, so she would just have to bite the bullet and tell her when she woke.

NELLY WAS SLOWLY WAKING. She had felt Ella get out of the bed and started to pull herself from slumber when she realized she didn't get back in. Nelly got up in somewhat of a panic. She had been sleeping hard, harder than usual, and felt an overwhelming sense of worry. She went to find her phone. It was in her purse and dead. She grabbed her charger and plugged it in, and caught sight of Ella on the balcony. Ella was sitting on the chair with her feet on the railing. She had her coffee in hand and appeared to be gazing off deep in thought. Nelly figured she would use the restroom before disturbing her. When her phone turned on, a series of texts bombarded her messages, causing it to glitch the notifications together. Ella heard it too and came back to the room. *The kids.* All of Nelly's worst fears shot through her mind like a bullet to the heart. The list of messages included everyone's name of the closest people to her, pretty much in succession. Her hand began shaking as she struggled to open any message.

"What is it?" Ella began to worry too. She could see the gentle bounce of Nelly's shirt on her chest, and a part of her started to panic too.

Nelly started opening the texts.

Nelly
Nelly
Yo, where are you?
Call me.
Now.
????
Nelly, call me when you get this.
You must be sleep already.
Call me, it's important.
Nelly, call me. Tres is in the hospital.

NELLY READ the series of text not realizing she had not taken a breath. The last one she read was from her mother. She looked at Ella. "Tres is in the hospital, I need to go." Nelly started moving quickly, frantically throwing clothes into her overnight bag.

"Hold on, slow down." Ella's brain was racing. She was going over the logistics. Nelly was supposedly out of town, checking on her mother.

"WHAT DO YOU MEAN SLOW DOWN, MY HUSBAND IS IN THE HOSPITAL." She checked herself, and said more calmly, "I need to go get him."

"Relax." Ella spoke softly. " All I'm saying is try to get some information on what happened before you go storming out here to rescue *your husband*. Besides, remember, you're 'not here' in California."

Nelly remembered and sat down on the edge of the bed to process. "Fuck!" She went to grab her phone and re-read through the texts.

"Did he call your mom?"

"I don't know. I mean someone did, she's been texting and calling me."

Ella's phone began pinging as well and she saw the notifications in her phone from the sports sites. She opened the one with Tre's name in the headline, "MLB All-Star Tres Dominguez found unconscious in his car, suspected overdose."

"Look." she walked over to Nelly, and put her hand on her shoulder. Nelly read the article and her eyes welled up with tears.

"I need to make sure he is ok."

"It says he's in stable condition. You want me to go with you?"

"No. It's best if I go alone. I will figure out my story... I'll call you later." With that she grabbed her bag and gave Ella a quick gentle kiss on the lips. There was no telling how this would unravel, but she had no choice but to find out.

Nelly called Maria first. She was worried the kids would hear something at school. It was 8:30am and Maria would just be dropping them off.

"Hello."

"Maria, I'm so glad I caught you. Where are the kids?"

"Here with me, at home. I saw the news this morning and wanted to wait until I heard from you before taking the children to school."

"Oh my gosh, thank you. I'm on my way to Tres. Thank you so much for thinking ahead. Keep them off the TV. I will call you when I know what's going on."

She hung up and dialed her mother next. She was trying to keep her focus on the drive, but knew she needed to handle as much as she could on this two hour drive.

"Mom."

"Nelly, oh my gosh baby, are you ok?"

"Have you talked to Tres?"

"No, what's going on? Are you ok?"

"Has he called you recently?"

"He called late last night, but I was sleep already."

"Good."

"What you mean, good? Nelly, what's going on?"

"I'll explain later Mom, Tres thinks I was with you, but please just don't talk to anyone until I call you back."

"Chanel, what do you mean he thinks you were with me? Explain now."

"Really, Mom, I can't. I need to figure out what's going on. I will call you back. Don't talk to anyone."

"Chanel!"

"Bye Mom." She hung up abruptly. She knew it would send her mom into a frenzy, but she told her enough for her mom to know to have her back no matter what was going on. In that way, Nelly and her Mom could always count on each other. Short and sweet was always code to trust and do what the other one was saying. A lot of times, it meant survival for them.

THE DOCTOR CAME into the room just as Tres was waking up. "Good morning Mr. Dominguez, feeling better?"

"Not really."

Tres was a wreck. Not only was his head pounding, but he still felt an immense amount of pain and tightness in his chest. He knew he fucked up this time, but couldn't recall the details of how he got there.

"Well you look much better than when you came in. I want to go over what happened, is that alright?"

Tre shook his head yes.

"EMT brought you in around 3:30 am. You were heavily sedated and had vomit on your clothes. Luckily, because you were seated upright in your car, you avoided a pretty deadly situation. We gave you a solution that contained activated charcoal through a feeding tube and hooked you up to some breathing machines. We've been running the IV to hydrate and clean you out. Do you have any idea what you took?"

"No, I was having some chest pain last night and I took some old pills I had that I thought were Xanax. That's kind of the last thing I remember."

"We are expecting the toxicology report back shortly, but any information can help us ensure we treat you properly. Also, just a heads up. There are some detectives here to ask a couple of questions. Don't feel like you have to tell them anything." With that, he gave Tres wink and let him know that he would be back in about an hour to check in on him. "Oh, and a gentleman named John, is in the waiting room. He said he's your agent. Should I send him back?"

"Yea, thanks."

John came in shortly after. His face displayed no emotion, like always. "Tres, what's good son?"

"Have you talked to Nelly?"

"I haven't been able to reach her. Her phone has been going straight to voicemail."

"Hijo de tu maldita madre." Tre became instantly agitated.

"I'm sure she will be calling back soon, she's probably on a flight back."

Tres started to get emotional again thinking about the photo from the night before. "She's not on a fucking flight man. She never left."

"What do you mean?" He could see Tres was getting worked up so he tried to keep him calm.

"Call that bitch ass Robert Patrick's agent. Tell him to ask Robert where she's

at." His fists were clenched and he started to get out the bed but stopped when he realized he was still hooked up to a few different machines. The realization made him even more upset. He felt trapped.

"Ok Tres, calm down man. Explain what's going on. I'm lost. I booked

Nelly on a flight to New York. I thought she was going to see her mom."

"Yea me too. So you can imagine my surprise when my boy sent me a

pic of her at some hotel bar way out in the desert somewhere."

"That doesn't sound right man."

Tres grabbed his phone and pulled up the picture of Nelly and Robert.

He handed it to John. John stared at the phone, trying to keep his composure for Tre's sake.

"I mean, are you sure this from last night?"

"Really, man?"

"Ok, ok. But listen Tres, we are going to have to deal with that later."

"Later? I don't fucking think so. Get that bitch ass Robert Patrick onthe phone right now."

"Ok Tres, I get it, but you need to try to calm down man. It's already a lot of heat, ok?"

Tres looked toward the window in attempt to hide his emotions. He was biting his lip, trying to hold back the tears. "I haven't been the best man to Nelly, everybody knows that. But I have always tried to do what I can to make up for that. And this last time, I was for real man. I was getting my shit together. I haven't done anything, not so much as even entertained a DM. Fucking Stacey was sweating my ass in Colorado and I ghosted her. I've been going to counseling. I've been spending more time with my kids." His fists were balled up.

"I know you have, Tres." It hurt him to see Tres this way and he was trying to be as comforting as possible, but he knew someone from the team would be there shortly. He needed him to pull it together. "Look, I have to tell you something you are not going to want to hear."

Tres kept his gaze towards the window as he wiped the few lines on his face. "I already know what you're going to say. I need to check into a facility. I know how these things go. How many days?"

"Well, we are going to report that it's for 30 days, and if you can do 14, that would be really good to show your commitment to getting better. We can switch to outpatient after that. You're looking at a 25 game suspension, which pretty much has you out until the end of the season, but if you do things right, you can be back for playoffs and make everyone forget about this.

But you're going to have to take it seriously this time, Tres. Your career is on the line. Everything you've worked for." Tres turned to look at him, gathering himself. He sniffed hard and nodded.

"Ok, I got this." He straightened himself out. He would have no choice but to deal with Nelly later.

"Now, I've had someone already make the arrangements for you to get admitted today. I think that's best. I will start doing some digging to figure out what's going on with Nelly. You need to focus on getting your mind right. I will let her know that you're at a facility."

"Don't tell her anything about the picture. And hire a private detective. I want her followed while I'm in there. Get her phone and card records too."

JOHN DIDN'T ANSWER Nelly's call until after the meeting with the team. By the time he answered she was only forty-five minutes away from the city. She went off as soon as he said hello.

"John, what the fuck! I've called you a hundred times. Where is Tres? Is he ok? Let me talk to him. I know you're with him. My calls aren't even going through to his phone."

"Nelly, just calm down."

"Don't tell me to fucking calm down. Where's my husband? I know he's in stable condition. Put him on the phone."

"I'm not with him anymore. I'm getting his paperwork in order for the facility. He has to check in Nelly." She got quiet for a moment.

"What happened? Where was he? Who was he with? How did this shit get out? Send me the address to the hospital."

"We can talk about all that later. He's getting transported in a few."

"Ok, then give me the address to the treatment place and I will meet him there."

"Nelly, he doesn't want to see you. He knows about your situation. His parents are on their way. They're going to come get the kids for a bit."

"What do you mean, my situation? And no the hell they aren't coming to get my kids. My children need to be with me, with us, me and Tres right now. What's the name of the place John?"

"He knows you've been seeing someone."

"John, I haven't…"

"Nelly, he knows." His tone was more firm than it had ever been with her.

"John, listen to me. Just let me see him. I need to talk to him."

"He needs to focus on his recovery. I think it's just best not to upset him anymore. Everything is depending on him completing this program. If he doesn't get it together, it's over for him. Please just lay low for a bit. I will call you when he's ready to see you." His voice was more gentle.

"This is fucking ridiculous. I'm his wife. And even if I was doing something that he thinks I am, after all he's put me through, he should at least be willing to talk to me."

"Nelly, trust me, ok. I will call you soon. Just lay low, ok? Don't talk to anyone." She hung up on him.

Nelly's hands were shaking. She could barely think straight. *What could he have seen or found out?* She thought to herself. They had been super careful. She began to wonder if maybe Ryan found out or if Ella told him. She did seem to always have a guilty conscience. Maybe she confessed. Maybe Robert did go back and say something. There were a million scenarios running through her head. Nelly called Ella, but she didn't pick up, so she messaged her.

Nelly: Ella, he knows.

Ella: Who?

Nelly: Tres, he knows about us.

Ella: How? Call me.

ELLA DIDN'T WAIT for her to call and dialed Nelly's number immediately.

"Hello."

"What do you mean he knows, how?"

"I don't know." Nelly started crying.

"Ok, just stay calm. He told you?"

"No, his agent. I called him to see what hospital Tres was at and he told me not to come. He said that Tres knows what I've been up to and it's best to just give him some space right now."

"Ok, let me think."

"Has Ryan said anything?"

"No."

"You didn't tell him right?" Nelly asked, unsure of how Tre would have found out.

"Are you fucking kidding me?"

"I know, sorry. I'm just freaking out. You think Robert went back and said something or told his wife or something?"

"I doubt it, he would have a lot of explaining to do."

"I know, but I just don't know how he would have found out."

"What about your friend, Laura. You said that's Tre's friend too."

"Yea, but no. She would never."

"You need to go talk to him and figure out what he knows." Ella said before taking a deep breath. "Look Nelly, we can't keep doing this."

"What are you talking about? Don't say that. I need you right now. Like, as my friend. Ok? Please."

Ella stayed quiet. She knew this thing had come to a head

and needed to be popped. If Tres did know, there was no telling how he would react or who he would tell.

"I'm pregnant, Nelly." She said it bluntly.

"What?" Nelly heard her, but she was sure she was mistaken. She heard Ella inhale and exhale.

"I wanted to tell you last night, but I just didn't know how to say it."

Nelly was silent. Tears began streaming down her face and she brought her fist to her mouth to try to control her breathing. Ella could hear her struggle.

"I didn't mean for any of this to happen Nelly. I'm so sorry, I..."

"Congratulations." Nelly cut her off. "You know a child is a blessing, no matter the situation." She had cleared her throat in attempt to manage, but Ella could hear her sniffles. "I'm happy for you."

"Nelly, I..."

"I need to go. I need to figure my shit out."

"Nelly, this doesn't mean we can't still talk you know, and be friends."

"Yea, I know. Goodbye Ella."

"I..." Nelly hung up. "Love you." The words landed on the sound of a dial tone.

NELLY FELT DIZZY. Her head was spinning and she felt faint. She couldn't even wrap her mind around what was happening. Why was everything crashing at once? She wanted Tres. He could always fix her problems, no matter how big or how small. And now, he didn't want to even see her. She refused to allow that. She sat down for a moment to breathe and gather her thoughts. Tres's mom. She hadn't even thought to call her, but she knew Tre wouldn't have said anything to his parents about this. Nelly called her mother-in-law and managed to get the address of the facility. She was right, Tres didn't mention to his parents that he didn't want Nelly there. He wouldn't want to explain why, especially to his dad who might consider disowning him at the thought of Tres allowing a woman to step out on him.

Nelly headed straight to the facility. It took her over an hour to get there with traffic. When she arrived, Tres had already checked in. The staff didn't hesitate to take her to his room. They opened his door to let her in, and left so they could have privacy. Tres rolled his eyes at the sight of her. She rushed over to him and tried to embrace him, but he blocked her with his arm.

"You got some nerve showing up here." She acted surprised.

"Tres, what's going on? No one would tell me where you were at or let me see you. Everyone was saying it was best for your recovery."

He wasted no time.

"Nelly, how could you? How could you fucking embarrass me like this. I get it, you trying to get me back, but at my job? I've never tried to disrespect you. I've always tried to mess with women that were the furthest from you, couldn't even touch you. If it wasn't for the damn internet, these thirsty hoes would stay in the black hole of the well they were trying to drink from, fucking invisible with no notoriety. But my teammate? My teammate Nelly? I mean I have to see him every day in person. Conyaso!"

Nelly was confused. *Robert?* Tres didn't even notice her surprise. He kept yelling, eyes full of tears. The occasional drop sneaking quickly down his face and met by his outer hand just as quickly, sweeping the wet off his face.

"And I knew it, I fucking knew it." He said as he punched one fist into his other hand. " I saw y'all look at each other and everything in me was saying something was up. You know

Nelly, in a way, I wasn't saying anything because I know I've put you through a lot over the years, and I was thinking, ok Nelly, just get it over with. Get me back so I can relax and stop looking over my shoulder wondering if you ever were going to need some sort of revenge."

"Him?" Nelly damn near whispered as not to upset him. He was staring out of the window of his room. Tres bit his lip and clenched his fist. His emotions were on a roller coaster, from sobbing to anger, to disbelief and her denial was sending him over the edge.

"Don't make it worse, mentirosa! I've never lied to you. Never!" He said through his teeth.

Nelly was scared. She had never seen him this unraveled before and had no idea how to correct him and assure him in this moment that it wasn't who he was thinking.

"Tres." She was like a mouse.

It made him take notice. He prepared himself for her to speak it and turned to look at her. He tried to change his tone.

"When did you meet him Nelly? At the charity event? This is why you've been having Maria around so much. When do you have time to meet up with him?" He thought back to the night, her dress, her sexiness, and how she had left him hanging that night. He was trying to remember when she would have talked to him, remembering that Robert was by them the entire evening, and he had only seen Nelly talking to Ella for the evening, after the other player wives had cornered her.

"Tres." She said it louder and firmer this time. He was ready to hear her say it.

"It's Ella."

"What?" He said it with an attitude, bothered that she would have the audacity to try to change the subject. "What about Ella?"

"It's Ella I've been seeing."

"Nelly, I fucking saw you with Robert! How can you continue to lie like this?"

"I know, but it's not him. If someone told you they saw me with him, it's because I was there with Ella and he was meeting up with her to discuss work." She figured she would keep his secret.

"Man, Nelly, you worst than me." He walked back towards the window. He was hurt that she wouldn't even come clean.

"Tres, I'm trying to tell you, I've been seeing Ella. Like *seeing* her."

He turned around, confused. "What do you mean?" It was starting to click. "Like fucking around?"

Nelly didn't want him to put it like that, but she shrugged and nodded yes. He walked to the bed and sat down. He was trying to piece it all together in his head. He stared at her. She was still sitting in the chair and was staring back. Her eyes began to fill with tears and she looked away.

"I don't even know what the fuck to say right now. Sooo...y'all are like a thing, or what?"

"No, I..., I mean, yes, but not like that anymore. It's over."

Tears began pouring out and she tried to breathe and keep her composure from the amount of pain she felt saying those words. The entire situation caught Tres off guard, but even more so, the fact that he could see how hurt she was.

He lowered his tone "You love her, Nelly?" It was more of a statement than a question. He hadn't seen her this pained since high school maybe. Part of him was relieved that it wasn't his teammate, but the other part didn't know what to feel. She had become so numb to his foolishness, that he never saw her feel that deeply in regards to him. It was a sting to see her toil over anyone else like that, but in the midst of that his instinct was to pick her up and hold her, console her and protect her. She looked so broken. He walked to her chair. "Come here." She looked up at him and his hands were stretched towards her summoning her to his arms. His compassion sucked the remaining strength out of her and she fell lifelessly into his embrace. He held her up in his hug, telling her that it was ok. He didn't understand her pain, but he understood her going astray. He always knew she would in some way, he was just glad it wasn't the way he imagined.

"We'll get through it. We will get through all of this Nelly. I'm going to make everything right, I promise."

The door swung open and the kids came running in followed by Tre's parents. They ran and wrapped their tiny arms around both of them. Nelly wiped her tears and smiled.

"Mami, why are you crying. Is Papi going to be ok?"

"Guela said he's sick!" Davida chimed in.

"Yea, I'm ok," Tre answered. "We all are. I'm going to be better real soon, I promise."

And just like that, Nelly held a small burial service for a piece of her soul. She wiped her eyes, pulled down her veil, and straightened her hat. She would have to continue wearing this one for now, it seemed to be the only one to fit, despite it's discomfort.